ZOMBIES
BOUGHT THE FARM

MARK FASSETT

ZOMBIES
BOUGHT THE FARM

MARK FASSETT

RAVENSTAR PRESS
MONROE, WA

Published 2013 by Ravenstar Press
Monroe, WA
www.ravenstarpress.com

Designed by Mark Fassett using StoryBox software
www.markfassett.com
www.storyboxsoftware.com

Cover Design by Mark Fassett

Images used:
© Chrisharvey | Dreamstime.com
© Deviney | Dreamstime.com

ISBN: 978-0615891101

For my wife,
who likes these
kinds of things.

1

I lay in bed, next to my fiancé, Brad, and stared out through the window of our confiscated farmhouse, our refuge for the last three months from a world overrun with zombies. All I could see through the window was the cold gray morning fog. If it was anything like the last week's weather, the fog would burn off by midday, turning the sky clear, but still cold.

I sat up. The chill in the house ate at my arms and my face, almost as if ice crystals had taken up residence.

I rubbed my face with my hands to warm up my cheeks. No ice crystals yet.

I glanced over at Brad, where he lay asleep, snoring. He had crawled into bed only hours earlier, after his shift on watch had ended. His hair had grown even longer than he had worn it three months earlier when the madness started. I liked it, though it did need a trim. He'd let his beard grow out, too. I didn't blame him. I found myself wishing I could grow a beard, just to keep my face warm.

Unfortunately, he still had his clothes on, as did I. It was the only way to keep warm in late November when you didn't dare light a fire.

Across the room, Danny, the ten-year-old boy we rescued that crazy night, still slept, too. He had his hand wrapped around the wrought iron fireplace poker we'd given him for defense. It wasn't a gun, but it was better than nothing. We didn't want him with a gun in his hand while he slept. He was covered in a pile of blankets we had scrounged up for him. It was one of the few nights he hadn't tried to squeeze his body into bed with Brad and I.

I slipped off the bed and tucked the covers back down around Brad. I felt like giving him a kiss and placed my lips on his forehead, light enough that he wouldn't be disturbed. He needed his sleep.

I went in search of Sean.

I found him sitting on the front porch, a sword in his hands, the shotgun propped up against the wall next to him. The ankle he had broken when jumping from his apartment balcony to the hood of the Humvee that first night had healed, for the most part. It still hurt him when standing or walking on it for too long. He tried to hide it, but could not keep the grimaces from his face. He had bundled himself in a thick, blue coat we'd found in the farmhouse. His face was just as scruffy as Brad's. I never thought I'd be living with mountain men.

"Andrea," he said, acknowledging me as I stepped out on the porch.

"Quiet?" I asked.

"Yep."

I looked out. It wasn't fog that kept the morning light gray. Thick, dark clouds carpeted the sky. By the looks of them, we were in for rain, or snow, if it was cold enough. I wished we had a thermometer, like I imagined most farmhouses did. The one that had hung outside the front door of our farmhouse had shattered long ago.

Off the front porch, within easy reach, sat the Hummer, for all the good it would do us. The fuel had run out a month earlier.

It was safer than the house, though.

"What do you think, Andrea? Are we going to sit here all winter?"

"I'm not sure what else we're going to do. We've got enough food, here," I said.

Brad wanted to go rescue his step-mom, the only person he had left in his family besides me, but we hadn't found a vehicle within walking distance that wasn't smashed, and finding fuel had proven problematic.

And we didn't even know if she was still alive. The phones had all died within two weeks of the zombie emergence.

"It doesn't feel right, just sitting here," Sean said.

"You sound as restless as Brad."

"I am. My ankle's mostly better, probably as good as it can get. We haven't seen a zombie in days. Maybe..."

"They're not gone," I said. "We're in the middle of nowhere out here. The cities will be teeming with them."

"I'm not saying we should go to the cities," Sean said. "I just think we should try to find some other survivors."

I couldn't help but laugh. "You just want your own girl."

Sean laughed, too. "It's not that funny. You and Brad, you get to share the warmth. It's cold sleeping alone."

"You could go sleep in the barn with the cows," I said. "It's always warm in there."

"Right. I smell bad enough as it is."

He did. We all did. The water wasn't running, either. We were surviving off bottled water and juice we'd scrounged from convenience and grocery stores.

The farm did have a hand pumped well, but the water came out pretty muddy, which meant we had to wait for the silt to settle before we could bathe in it. Most of the time, we just didn't bother. What I wouldn't give for a hot shower, but feeling clean wasn't exactly worth the effort, the wait, or the chill of an unheated bath.

We hadn't dared to drink the water ourselves, but we did pump it for the cows. We had decided to keep them alive as long as we could, hoping that someone would happen along that might know how to milk or butcher them.

It had surprised us, when we arrived, that the cows were still out in the fields munching on grass. It took a few encounters and a bit of observation before we noticed that the zombies seemed to avoid them. They pretty much avoided anything that wasn't people.

"What's for breakfast?" I asked.

"Breakfast?"

"Yeah," I said. "It's your turn. I'm tired of making breakfast."

Sean laughed. "You know I can't cook."

"Fine, give me the shotgun, you go get the eggs."

Brad had been right about finding a farm. It had taken us longer than we had anticipated to find one that wasn't burned out, looted, or so covered in blood that you couldn't even breathe inside.

When we finally found this one, with the Hummer almost out of fuel for the fortieth time, it had come with a bonanza of farm animals, including the aforementioned cows, and chickens. Dozens and dozens of chickens.

They'd all be dead, soon. We were running out of feed and we were down to the last eight. Once we realized we'd lose them all at once, we started killing and eating them. I hated all the plucking that was necessary, but after a couple tries, it didn't turn out too bad, and it beat canned beans every night.

It would be time to slaughter another one soon, but not today.

"Fine," Sean said, "I'll go get the eggs."

He stood up and handed the shotgun to me. He kept the sword for himself and stepped off the porch.

Right after I heard the first crunch of dirt from his heel, I thought I heard a low hum, like that of a motor.

"Stop, Sean."

"What?"

"Shhh."

He stopped.

The motor sound disappeared. Whatever it was, it had been far away.

We waited in silence for a few moments.

I heard the chickens clucking away in the coop, though, and a cow chose that moment to throw out a plaintive moo.

I just about told him to go get the eggs when the sound came back. It was louder, now, and clearly a motor, a vehicle motor.

"Forget the eggs," I said. "Wake up Brad and Danny."

Even with the urgency that might be necessary, you didn't shout. You never knew how far away the zombies were.

Sean clambered back up onto the porch and hurried inside.

I stepped off the porch and ran for the Humvee. It might not go anywhere, but the gun still worked.

This was our fucking farm, and I was not about to let someone come in and take it without a fight.

2

We didn't have much ammo left for the big gun, a dozen rounds at most, but our visitors wouldn't know that. The gun had been a lifesaver when Brad's father used it and some quick thinking to extract me from the nightmare my apartment had become. Unfortunately, he had used up most of the rounds.

On our trip to the rural areas north of Seattle, we had conserved what we could. We weren't likely to find any more ammo for the gun. We had stumbled across a couple of gun shops on our trip, but they had been stripped bare. The weapons we had were pretty much it, unless we could get back to Brad's father's place, or we got lucky and stumbled across an abandoned survivalist compound—where the word abandoned means the people turned into zombies and left, leaving their weapons behind.

Brad thought we might find one or two out here, but we had had no luck.

The sound of the motor grew louder.

I swiveled the gun around to point down the gravel encrusted driveway. I had a quarter mile of unobstructed view to the road, a two lane strip of pavement that wound along the base of a tree covered hill. That quarter mile would give me more than enough time to decide whether or not to open fire on our visitors, should they decide to turn down the driveway.

And I didn't doubt they would at least think about it. They weren't driving fast. They were looking for something.

The door to the house opened behind me, and feet rumbled on the porch. I chanced a peek and saw Sean and Brad and their weapons. Brad was still rubbing at his eyes with one hand, but carried a sword in the other. Despite my efforts to teach him, he was still useless with a gun. He hadn't really mastered the sword, either, but he'd become proficient at dispatching zombies with it, and for the most part, that's all that mattered.

It worried me. I would have preferred he take them out at a distance, but he couldn't hit anything farther away than about ten feet.

He looked up at me and pursed his lips into a kiss.

God, I loved him. He was always thinking of me.

I just wished he could shoot.

The sound of the motor grew suddenly louder, and I spun back around. It wasn't a car at all. A school bus, painted white and gray, emerged from behind a copse of trees beyond the cow pastures. Even from where I was, I could see that the windows were either painted or armored.

"Shit," Brad said.

"What?" I asked, even though I felt the same way. A

bus could be carrying a lot of people.

"It's a prison bus," he said.

"Damn," I said. "Get off the porch. Where's Danny?"

"I left him asleep," Sean said.

"Go get him," I said. Leaving Danny alone in the house during this confrontation was only a marginally worse idea than having him with us, but if we had to run, I wasn't leaving him behind.

Brad jumped off the front porch to crouch behind the Humvee. Sean ran back inside.

I ducked down into the Humvee.

The last thing we needed was to have a bus full of ex-cons see us and think we were easy prey. We weren't, but it would be better off if they didn't see us at all. It made me wish we could hide the Humvee and its gun, but it was too late for that.

I found myself wishing Brad was in the Humvee with me. He could drive, I could shoot. We could take out that bus without a problem, if only we had fuel.

The shooting would draw zombies, though. Hell, the sound of that bus was likely to draw a few.

The bus slowed as it approached the turn to our driveway.

They were thinking about it.

They were probably looking for loot, and if that's what they were looking for, we had it.

The bus came to a stop.

I opened a compartment behind the front seats and pulled out a pair of binoculars.

With the closer view, I could see that the bus was definitely armored with something, but there was no logo on the side. I couldn't see very well through the door, as it was armored, too, but I saw well enough to see a shadow move inside. They were scoping us out, or at least, checking out the Humvee. They were probably looking for activity.

The bus rolled forward, and then it made a slow turn into our driveway.

Hiding had not been the answer.

I pushed myself back up into the sling for the gun and showed myself.

"Come out, Brad," I said.

Now that they had rolled down our driveway, we needed to show them we weren't to be fucked with.

3

As soon as I popped up and manned the gun, the bus stopped. It had driven perhaps a quarter of the way down the driveway. If I had more rounds, I could have lit it up, though the dozen I had would do a bunch of damage. Of course, they didn't know how low we were, and I was pretty sure the front window of the bus was not armored.

"What do you think they're doing?" Brad asked.

"Waiting."

I loved the way he deferred to me in these kinds of things. He was a computer geek and smarter than hell, but when it came to understanding people, he could be a bit dense.

I heard the sound of a window open off to my left. A glance in that direction showed me that Sean was ready. His head wasn't visible from where I sat, but his rifle was poking out of the window. I didn't see Danny, but I suspected he would be right there next to Sean with a pistol in his hand. Even at ten years old, Danny was better with a gun than Brad would ever be.

"I hope they fucking make up their minds," Brad said. "I want breakfast."

So did I.

The engine on the bus shut off.

They weren't leaving right away.

Then the bus rocked a little, and a man stepped out.

I pulled up the binoculars to get a good look at him.

For some reason, I had expected to see a uniform, either that of a cop or security guard, or that of a prisoner, but this guy came out wearing a blue plaid shirt and denim jeans. He looked to be in his early fifties and wore rimmed glasses with round lenses which were held up by a beak of a nose. The top of his head grew salt and pepper hair that was just starting to thin. He held up a white something-or-other in his hand, and it took me a moment to realize it was a bra.

Whatever works, I guess.

He walked slowly toward us waving the bra. His eyes darted everywhere, including occasional glances in my direction.

I knew what he feared, being out in the open without a weapon.

"Sean," I called out. "Leave Danny with the rifle and get down here."

I heard a noise at the window, but I kept my eye on the man from the bus.

Whoever was in that bus, I no longer thought they were prisoners.

"What are you thinking?" Brad asked.

"Time to go meet him, see what he wants. I'll have Sean man the Humvee, and you and I will go for a walk."

"Right. You know you're fucking crazy," he said.

It made me smile. It was an oft repeated term of endearment from him, especially over these last three months.

"Maybe this guy's a preacher," I said, "and we can finally get married."

Brad laughed. It was a rare sound these days.

"Well, then, I guess you are right. We should go talk to him."

Sean emerged from the house and walked over to the Humvee. The man had not yet reached the half-way point between the bus and us. My bet was that he would stop there.

"Take the gun up here," I said to Sean.

"You're going to meet him?" he asked.

"Why not? I doubt they have much food, but I bet they have fuel. Maybe we can trade. Maybe there's a woman in there for you, too."

Sean rolled his eyes. "Right. Come down from there." His voice had a little more hope in it than I'd heard in a while, though.

I climbed out, took the shotgun with me, and handed the binoculars to him.

"If anything happens, don't shoot the guy, shoot that bus," Brad said.

Brad took my hand. He had sheathed his sword and strung it across his back. I held the shotgun pointed to the ground.

I wasn't as brave as that old guy. I wasn't going to go out there unarmed.

"Shall we go?" Brad asked.

He squeezed my hand.

"Yes," I said. "Let's go meet our pastor."

Brad laughed again, and then we walked.

4

The man had stopped just about the midway point between his bus and the Humvee. He waited for us in that *ready to run* stance that we had all seemed to adopt. Maybe 'act' was a better word than 'run'. We certainly hadn't run from zombies in a long time.

People, however, they have mostly been downright nasty. Who survives the zombie apocalypse? People that are willing to fight and aren't too stupid to live. A large number of those people are not very nice.

We'd been fortunate that we had always had the bigger gun, so far.

The man didn't call out to us as we approached. He waited to say something until we came to a stop with a nice safe distance between us. He had learned. Quiet is safe. Loud is dead.

"Hello," he said, taking the initiative.

I stood silent, and Brad took my cue.

"I'm Randy," he said.

"Randy," said Brad.

"What's in the bus, Randy?" I asked.

He inadvertently glanced back at the bus.

"My family," he said.

"No one has family anymore," I said. For some reason, I was thinking of my dad. I hadn't heard from him in months even before the nightmare started. He'd run off to Vegas or Acapulco or somewhere. He had every right. I was an adult and living on my own, but it felt like I'd been abandoned nonetheless.

"You sure you're not criminals?" Brad asked.

The man's eyes grew wide.

"What? No. What makes you think that?"

"You're driving a prison bus," Brad said.

"Oh, that. We found it outside of Bellingham, took it for our own."

I didn't care about the bus.

"How many inside?" I asked.

"Eight."

"I don't believe it," said Brad.

Randy looked at Brad sternly. The man may have been nervous about his surroundings, about meeting us, but he obviously didn't take kindly to being called a liar.

Call me foolish, but I liked him.

"You don't believe what, young man?"

A teacher. He had to be. A professor up at Western Washington University, perhaps.

"I don't believe that you saved seven members of your family," Brad said.

Brad had a point. It was unlikely at best. But then,

perhaps it had gone down differently in Bellingham than it did in Lynnwood.

"It wasn't easy. I lost six," he said.

Holy shit. How big was this guy's family?

"Someone is in there watching, right? Have them step out. We need to see," I said.

"But..."

"Look, I want to believe you, and if you're telling the truth, we aren't going to hurt you, but you have to admit that the bus looks just a bit creepy. If you were in our position, you'd want to see who you were dealing with."

"I can understand that. I just don't think it's wise to have them all get out," he said.

"Oh, you're worried about zombies?"

He nodded, and nervously looked around again.

"Don't worry too much. We haven't seen a zombie in a week. They're few and far between, here, and there's a lot of land between us and the nearest shelter. They'll have time to get back on the bus," I said.

"I still don't..."

I caught a glance from Brad, and knew he was thinking Randy was hiding something from us. I was beginning to feel the same way.

"Look Randy," I said, intentionally loosening up my shotgun arm, "you seem like the trustworthy type, but I've seen enough shit these last three months that I don't take too many people at their word. If you don't empty it out, I'll have Sean, back there, empty it out for you with that gun."

"Alright, alright," he said, then he turned around. I bet he was wishing he had just passed on by this place, but I knew it was hard to resist. We had stopped there ourselves.

Randy waved his hands and a man just a little older looking than Brad poked his head out of the driver's side window. All I could really see was a mass of brown curls.

"Everybody out," Randy yelled.

"You sure?"

"Yes."

"Okay, that's enough yelling," I said. Sure, we hadn't seen a zombie in a week, but it didn't mean they weren't out in the forest somewhere.

And then Randy's family started piling out of the bus.

First, an older woman, about the same age as Randy, I guessed.

"Name them off as they come out," I said.

"Fine. That's my wife, Barb," he said.

The next one out was even older. "My mom." No actual name, but I let it slide.

Then, in short order, a younger woman and two young children, boy and girl. "My daughter-in-law, Izzy and my grandchildren Katrina and Andrew."

The man with the big mop of curls that had stuck his head out the window followed them out.

"My son, Derrick."

A younger man, probably no more than twenty, and a young woman that looked to be my age were the last to step off the bus. "My other son Brian, and my daughter Emma."

"That's it?" Brad asked.

"Yes."

"So," I said, "why did you stop?"

"We're running low on food. We saw the cattle, thought to butcher us one or two."

My hopes just went up. The thought of steak made my

stomach very happy.

"You know how to butcher a cow?" Brad asked.

"Derrick does. He worked as a butcher."

"One last question," I said.

Randy blinked at me as if to hurry me up.

"Where are you going?"

"We have a place on the other side of the mountains. It was to be our refuge in case war broke out or something."

"Survivalist?" Brad asked.

"Pragmatist," Randy said. "Unfortunately, the zombies came without warning."

That was certainly the truth. From normal to devastation in the course of one day.

I pulled Brad to me and whispered to him. "What do you think?"

"It's more mouths, more chances for shit to go wrong," he said. That was one thing I was unhappy with about Brad. That first night, he had saved me, saved Sean, saved Danny and Danny's mom, but since then, he seemed to have turned on strangers. Losing both his parents that day hadn't soured him immediately, but as the weeks passed and we had been unable to get back to Lynnwood to keep his promise to his step-mother his desire to help people had seemed to turn more to despair. It didn't help that most people we had met since had turned out to be shit-holes.

But this was too good to pass up.

"If they butcher some meat for us, it won't affect our food levels. More hands means more work gets done, and maybe, just maybe, they might have some extra fuel. Maybe we can go back and help your step-mother."

Brad looked at Randy for a moment, who was watching us intently. He could probably hear our whispers.

Then Brad turned back to me.

"It's up to you," he said.

Fine. If it was up to me, we were having fresh steak for dinner.

"Get them all back in the bus and pull it up next to the Humvee. Then have everyone step out again, and just to be sure that we didn't accidentally miss anyone, you and Brad are going to do a walk-through of the bus when we get there.

"Once we're certain you're not putting us on, I think your son should get to butchering us a cow so we can eat a decent meal tonight."

"Thank you," Randy said.

"Oh, one other question," I said.

"What?"

"You wouldn't happen to be a pastor, would you?"

5

"No, I'm no pastor," Randy said. "I'm a philosophy professor."

I consoled myself that my first guess about his occupation had been on target. However, if there was ever an area of study that I would have thought completely useless after the zombie apocalypse, it would have been philosophy.

But somehow, he had done better than we had. He still had less than fifty percent casualties.

Randy and his family followed our instructions without any complaints. We did have the bigger guns, but I suspected their obedience had more to do with the philosopher side of him than any bad-assedness on our part.

When Brad checked out the bus, he found only what Randy had told us was there. An extra tank of fuel, a few weapons, and food that probably wouldn't last them the week. No surprise that the farm enticed them.

Once that was done, Brad shook hands with Randy and smiled.

"Sorry about all that," Brad said. "I've seen one too many zombie movies. Shit, we've all been living one for the last three months."

"We understand," Randy said.

"Which of your sons was it that knew how to butcher a cow?"

"I do," said Derrick. Up close, his hair wasn't quite the mop that it looked like when he leaned out of the bus window.

"Why don't we go get us one," Brad said. "I've been hungry for a steak since the day I set eyes on them."

Derrick looked at his father, and Randy nodded his head.

Brad came over to me and gave me a kiss. "I'm going to take Danny for a lookout," he said.

I don't know what prompted the kiss, but I liked it enough that I wasn't going to argue with him.

"Brian," Randy said, "go with them."

"Okay," said Randy's younger son.

He looked a lot more like Randy than Derrick did. Thin, straight hair, the same beak of a nose. He wore a faded Dresden Dolls t-shirt that covered a fairly muscular body. He and I probably would have been friends had I attended college with him.

"Should I take a weapon?" Brian asked.

"Always," I said. "We may not have seen a zombie in a week, but it doesn't mean they aren't out there."

He pulled a thick metal pipe, about the length of Brad's sword, out from under the bus. The four of them headed off for the barn, leaving Sean and I to manage the other five.

"Are you going to be wanting to sleep in the house?" I asked.

Randy glanced at the house and quickly looked back at me.

"No, I don't think so," Randy said.

I didn't blame him. If it was at all comfortable to sleep in the Humvee, we wouldn't be sleeping in the house, either.

"Well, let's head inside, anyway, and see what we can do about something to go with our meat." My mouth watered just thinking about the taste of a good steak.

Eight hours later, the ten of us were sitting around a candle-lit table eating goat instead of beef, and Sean sat outside in the dim gray of a cloud covered twilight eating his own meal while keeping watch. I had known the goats were out there, but I hadn't even thought of eating them. It turned out that once Derrick saw the goats, he suggested them over a cow because the cow would take so much more time to butcher, and they'd end up wasting a lot of it.

Secretly, though I thought the goat was pretty good, I didn't care if they wasted a lot of the cow. There weren't exactly a lot of people around to eat them, anyway.

The company around me was quiet. I still don't think Randy trusted us much, and I sure as hell didn't trust him as much as I wanted to. He seemed like a nice guy, as far as people like us went—us meaning zombie apocalypse survivors—but we hadn't run into very many nice guys.

I tried to prod Brad into talking with my eyes, figuring that Randy might be more comfortable talking with him, but I don't think our telepathy was working. He either ignored what I wanted, or didn't understand.

Eventually, I couldn't take the quiet any more.

"Where is this hideout of yours, Randy?" I asked.

Randy looked up from his plate, his fork hanging out of his mouth. Slowly, he removed the fork.

"It's near Lake Chelan," he said.

"Good place for fishing?" I asked.

He nodded. "Hunting, too."

I'd been to Lake Chelan when I was a kid. I recall hearing that it was the longest lake in Washington.

Four months ago, I would have looked it up on the internet. I used to hate it when I couldn't be sure I had my facts straight.

"Don't you think Chelan will have its share of zombies?" Brad asked. He'd read my mind.

"We're up the lake quite a ways," Randy said. "Not many people up that far at all."

"But the resorts would have been full of tourists and campers, back when the zombies broke out."

"It's possible," Derrick broke in, "but we can handle it. We just have to get to the boat launch, and then we're as good as home."

Randy stared daggers across the table at his son.

No, Randy still didn't trust us, not completely.

I decided to ignore it. We weren't going there, anyway, not yet, and not with them. "So you'll be taking Highway 2 over Stevens Pass?" I asked.

"It seems the best choice," Randy said.

There are three real options over the mountains: North Cascades Highway, Highway 2, and I-90. I know the North Cascades Highway closes every year due to snow as it becomes practically impossible to traverse. Highway 2 often closes, too, but would reopen as soon as they cleared it. Of course, without the snow plows running, it might be impassable.

As I thought about it, I started to wonder about his plan. Getting stuck up in the snow on the mountains in November was a likely possibility.

Brad apparently came to the same conclusion.

"Why did you wait so late to try to cross the passes?" Brad asked. "I'm sure they've all seen snow by now. You're likely to get stuck up there."

"We didn't have any choice," Derrick said.

Randy stuck his arm out toward his son, finger extended. "Derrick," he said, in an effort to silence his son.

"Dad, they need to know," Derrick said.

At this point, Brad sat up, and I did the same. I looked around the table quickly, and caught looks of worry on the face of Randy's wife and his daughters.

"What do we need to know?" I asked.

Randy and Derrick locked themselves in a staring contest. I might have found it amusing if I didn't think our lives might hang in the balance. Of course, these days, our lives always hung in the balance.

"What do we need to know?" I asked again, this time pounding the table with my fist to try to emphasize my impatience.

But they met my insistence with silence.

Tense moments passed while they stared at each other,

Derrick clearly wanting to tell us something, but not yet ready to flout his father's will.

I looked at Brad, and he had one hand on the table, the other had slid beneath it. From the angle of that arm, I guessed he'd placed it on the pommel of his sword.

I think he had the same thought I did.

Danny, sitting on my right, was looking at me, waiting for instructions.

"If you don't tell us what Derrick thinks we need to know," Brad said while getting to his feet, "then I think it's time you leave."

It made me proud. He was no longer the man-geek that spent all his time in front of his computer. He still couldn't hit anything smaller than the broad side of a car with a gun, but he no longer took crap from anyone except me.

Both Derrick and Randy turned to look at Brad, and they saw what I saw. Brad's face was cold, unemotional. His hand was indeed resting on the pommel of his sword, and he was ready to draw it, should the need arise.

"Now, young man," Randy said, "there's no need for that."

"Then tell us what you're hiding."

Randy opened his mouth as if to say something, but he didn't get a chance.

The sound of a shotgun shell exploded into the room from outside the front window, followed immediately by a single shouted word from Sean.

"Zombies!"

7

I grabbed Danny and pulled him toward the window. It wasn't exactly the reaction you would expect from a normal woman in a crisis, but I knew Brad would be working his way to the front door to help Sean, and we needed Danny's gun. He had become a good shot, and frankly, I did not think shielding him from the horrors of our new world would do anyone any favors.

I paid no attention whatsoever to our guests. We had made them leave their weapons in the storage bins on the bus. Maybe that's what had them nervous. Whatever, it didn't matter then. All that mattered was killing zombies.

I didn't need to slide the window open. There were already squares of glass missing from the subdivided window.

The light from the candles on the table reflected in the glass, making it hard to see.

"Put the candles out!" I shouted.

The candles went out quick.

Beyond the window, beyond our vehicles, about a half dozen of the upright dead loped toward us, shadows in the night. They would have been invisible to me if not for the rarity of a clear sky and a half moon. Nothing we couldn't take care of, but worrisome. Where did that many come from? We hadn't seen more than one or two at a time in weeks. And, the bigger question: were there more out there?

A little closer, one writhed on the ground where it had fallen after Sean put it down. We'd finish it later. The first task was to get them all on the ground.

Someone came to stand beside me.

"How many?" Derrick asked.

Not Randy. Interesting.

"Not too many," I said.

I stuck the barrel of my pistol through a hole in the window, pulled the trigger. The closest one tumbled to the ground. My father had trained me pretty well, and I'd only improved in the last three months.

"One less, now." I said.

Danny shot, too, the report of his gun banging through the dining room. His target fell to the ground right next to mine.

My ears started to ring. They were doing that far too often, lately. It would have been nice to have some ear protection, like we had at the firing range.

Another shot from Sean stopped the progress of a third zombie, and then we had to stop shooting.

Brad raced off the porch, his sword held high like you see in cheesy samurai movies. I don't know if that stance was effective against humans with swords. I doubted it.

But against zombies, it set him up for the killing stroke every time.

One, two, three, the heads of the remaining zombies went flying as he sliced through their necks with that sword. He never showed that side of himself when we were first dating, but ever since that first night, he had become death to zombies with that sword, as long as he had space to fight in.

Bullets ran out.

His sword never did.

And he was only getting better with it, at least when it came to zombies.

"He's good with that sword," Derrick said.

"He's had a lot of practice," I said.

"There will be more," Derrick said in a whisper.

"More?" I asked.

"They are following us," he said, again in a whisper.

With the ringing in my ears, I wasn't sure I heard him right.

But when he was abruptly dragged backward, I knew I had.

I spun, gun held out, pointed at Randy, who had his son by the collar of his shirt, and a steak knife in his hand.

Randy's other son Brian stood behind him, holding a knife of his own. The women had backed away, but they all held their own knives.

Even with my gun, with Danny there, I didn't feel the odds were in my favor.

"Brad!" I shouted. "Get in here!"

And then, as calmly as I could, I asked, "Why are they following you, Randy?"

Randy returned to the table and fell into a chair. His behavior and demeanor was completely confusing to me. One moment, he seemed adamant that they not tell us anything, holding a knife in front of him and threatening Danny and I with it, and not two minutes later, he was sitting in that chair, head hung, clearly pondering telling me everything, defeated.

He was tired, I think. Tired of running.

"Why, Randy?" I asked again.

"I don't know. A week ago, a flood of them came from the north, maybe out of Canada. We were just outside of Bellingham at the time, far enough from the city to avoid the majority of the dead that still roam Bellingham's streets, but close enough to make runs for supplies."

Randy lifted his head, seemingly staring at me, but in the shadows, they felt dead. I'm not sure he was looking at me.

"We had radio contact with friends near the border. A week and a half ago, they went silent. We started preparations to leave, but kept hope that they would come back. We thought maybe they had run out of batteries, though they said nothing about that to us. Our bigger worry was that bandits had overrun them.

"We were wrong."

I waited for him to say more, but my mind was already working. A large wave of zombies coming south. From where? Canada. Vancouver.

But why? The cold? That didn't seem likely. I wouldn't have imagined them to have that much thought in their dead brains. I hadn't thought they had any real intelligence left at all, or that they would be afraid of anything. They were pure hunger, from what I had seen.

I heard footsteps outside the room, and then Brad stepped through the entryway.

"What happened?" I asked.

"There were only a few at first," Randy said. "We thought it was just a small group, but with our friends having gone silent, I was nervous. I moved everyone to the bus, just in case. I'm glad I did."

Brad looked confused, but he didn't interrupt Randy.

"We had a fence around our property, chain-link, eight feet high. It kept out the dead until then. To the north of us, there was a low hill."

I noticed Randy shudder. I looked around the room at the others. Randy's mother was playing oblivious, but the others listened intently, eyes wide, like they were seeing what had happened to them all over again. Perhaps they were. I'm certain it was still fresh in their minds.

"About six hours after we slaughtered the first group, zombies swarmed over the hill. Hundreds of them, maybe thousands, just after daybreak. The fence withstood them for no more than a few seconds."

"And the zombies we just slew?" Brad asked, his voice cold.

"Maybe just a random group," Randy said.

"And maybe," Brad said, walking in between Randy and I, then turning to face Randy. I noticed, as he walked, that his sword was still out, covered with the ichor of the dead. "Maybe, it's a forerunner group. Maybe you've dragged them here. Maybe the reason you don't want to sleep in the house was because you were planning to leave in the middle of the night without telling us what was coming our way."

"No," said Randy, but I could see it in his face. I could see it in the nervousness of the others.

Brad tapped the sword against the floor, spraying black drops down upon it. I feared Brad was angry enough to kill Randy, to try to take them all on.

I glanced over at Danny. He looked worried, his forehead creased, but he had his gun out. He was prepared.

Brad raised the sword, set the tip of it on Randy's chest.

"Yes, right? Don't lie to me."

Randy nodded.

"Good," Brad said. "Good of you to admit it. However, there's a price for trying to fuck us."

"What?"

"How much fuel do you have in that thing?"

"No," Randy whispered.

"Don't worry. We don't want all of it. Just half. Enough to get us just as far as you."

"Please," Randy said.

"You should have been straight with us. We're all fucking human still. We let you in instead of shooting you up. We let you eat with us. And you were going to repay us by leaving us to die. You're damned lucky we don't take all of it."

From the sound of Brad's voice, he was damned lucky Brad didn't run him through right there.

9

Brad took Randy's son Derrick out with him to transfer the fuel from the bus to the Humvee. He left me and Danny in the room with the rest of Randy's family after he collected the steak knives and dropped them out the front window.

Staring at them, watching them sit in their chairs with nervous looks on their faces while we waited, took as much of my nerve to handle as facing a horde of zombies. Brad was right. They were getting better than they deserved, but I didn't like it. I couldn't help but think we were setting them up to die.

I couldn't wait to get going.

And I couldn't let the silence go on any longer. It was getting to be too much.

"Why do you think the zombies are coming this way?" I asked Randy.

"I don't know. I thought the cold, or lack of..."

"People to eat?"

"Maybe. I don't know. We have to get out of here."

"You know, if you had told us, we could have all been moving on before now, and you wouldn't be here under the guns of four pissed off people."

"We didn't know you," he said.

"You knew we were alive," I said, my anger getting the best of me. "Brad... Brad and his father risked their lives to come save me, then they saved Danny and his mom, and then Sean. They didn't have to. They could have stayed home, tried to save themselves. Instead, they chose to save whoever they could. And you..."

"Things have changed," Randy said with his eyes on the floor.

"Things haven't changed," I said. "I mean, yeah, the zombie thing, that changed. But if we don't help who we can, we lose all of us. I think what's got Brad so upset is that you looked like nice people. You looked like the kind of people he would want to help."

His mother, spoke up, then, for the first time all night. "We *are* nice people."

"Nice people don't leave people to die," said Danny. His voice wavered. I think he was remembering his mother at that moment. I wanted to bend down and give him a hug, but that was impossible. I had to watch these people, and Danny did, too.

Not long after, Brad shouted through the window, "Time to go."

I skirted the room, pulling Danny along with me, watching all of their heads turn to follow me.

"Randy," I said, once I got to the door safely. "You can

come out once you no longer hear the Hummer, but not 'til then. We see you come out before we're gone, I swear I'll mow you all down. People like you are turning people like Brad and I into people like you. Good luck on your trip."

Danny and I hurried out to the Humvee, which Brad had already started up, and climbed in.

Brad put it in gear and off we went.

I watched until I couldn't see the farm any longer. But I did see them come out just as we left the driveway.

We weren't going to shoot them. Couldn't afford to waste the ammo.

10

"How much fuel do we have," I asked, once we were on the road.

Night had fully descended, bringing the darkness of a cloud covered sky down upon us. The only light came from the lone, still working headlight on the Humvee. We'd never found a replacement for the other.

"A full tank," Brad said. "The back of that bus was full of fuel cans."

"I thought you had told me there was only one extra tank."

"I thought so, too. They squirreled away all these tiny one and two gallon cans behind it, anywhere they would fit. I missed them the first time around."

I didn't want to ask how he found them the second time around.

"So where are we going?" I asked, instead.

Brad turned to me for just a moment, looked at me as if trying to judge whether he should answer the question truthfully. Because of that, I knew the answer before he said it.

"To get my step-mom."

"It's been too long," I said.

"She'll still be alive. I promised we'd come back. I'm not just going to abandon her."

No, he wouldn't abandon anyone, at least not anyone that hadn't just pissed him off. One of his best, and most frustrating qualities.

"And if Lynnwood is overrun? If the house is overrun? What then? We'll have wasted the fuel getting there when we could have used it to go somewhere else."

"You'd have me forget about her? I promised, Andrea. I promised. Besides," Brad said, "there's another reason to go."

"Yeah?"

"My dad's place will have more ammo for the gun. For all of them."

I tried. I wasn't going to stop him if he thought it was important. And his second point did make a lot of sense.

"And afterward?"

"Maybe the wave of zombies won't come that far," he said. "Maybe we can stay there."

"Stay there? You can't be serious. I thought I was the psychotic one."

"It's safe, it's got the fence."

"Your step-mom said there were too many zombies for *them*. You can't even shoot, and inside that house, if the zombies are still there, it'll be..."

Sean's the smart one. He stayed out of this fight, even after the silence dragged on for minutes.

"It'll be what?" Brad asked.

"Look, we can go. You're right. We should at least check on your step-mom, and we need the ammo and whatever supplies might be there, if it's not picked over by now. But we are *not* staying there. I want..."

"You want what?"

That was when I realized I wanted what I couldn't have. I wanted it all to go back to normal. I wanted to go back to being PsychoAndrea. I wanted to go back to a normal world where normal shit happened, where people didn't show up on your doorstep dragging half the zombie-world down on top of you and then try to pretend that they didn't do it.

"I wanna go back and shoot those fuckers that drove us off our farm," I said. I couldn't let him know I was breaking. Not right then. Not in the middle of a fight.

"We can't," Brad said.

"I know we can't. It doesn't mean I want it any less."

I peered out the window and Brad returned to driving. He glanced at me once or twice, I think, but I kept my attention on the outside world.

We couldn't just drive down the road. While it wasn't quite littered with dead cars like most of the freeways, there were enough obstacles that Brad had to drive with caution, weaving around them. Burned out or dead vehicles accounted for most of the obstacles, but occasionally, downed trees or power lines caused us headaches and delays as we had to find alternate routes around the blockages. All the while, Brad bitched about how much fuel the detours were costing us. Thank God the GPS system still worked, though I didn't doubt it would be long before the satellites started falling from the sky.

The drive was nice, though, despite it all. Far better than the first hellish days after it all came down.

I looked over at Brad and his bearded face that was spending so much effort concentrating on his driving.

Maybe he was right.

Maybe the worst of it was over and the zombies had migrated away, looking for new food.

That thought reminded me of the other threat. The horde from Canada. What if...

"Brad?"

"Huh?"

"You don't think that horde they talked about will come this far, do you? Like, to your Dad's house?"

"No idea. I hope not." He sounded like the idea worried him, though.

"What if they are coming south," I said, "not because it's cold, but because they're hungry. What if everyone in Canada is dead?"

"Not everyone in Canada is dead," Brad said. "That's just too many people. There have to be some survivors."

And then I voiced the thought that really had me worried. "What if we run into a horde that's coming north from Seattle? What if..."

"Why are you worrying so much?"

"Your father's place might be a good place to ride it out, maybe. But I realized that we're sort of stuck here. The zombies are stuck here, between the mountains and the ocean for hundreds and thousands of miles."

"And you think that if we stay at my dad's place, that we'll eventually be overrun."

"I do."

Just the thought of a thousand zombies or more up against the fences was enough to make me shiver. And we didn't even know how many zombies we were talking about. There were four million people in Western Washington, alone. My bet was that ninety percent of those were now dead and walking.

My eyes caught a shadow, about a hundred feet in front of us, shambling along, attracted by the sound of the Humvee, or the lone headlight.

"Zombie," I said.

"I got it," Brad said.

The Humvee thumped only a little as Brad drove over the zombie. He never missed a chance to take out his frustrations on them.

"Okay," he said after we left the flattened zombie behind. "I see your point. We won't stay at my dad's place any longer than necessary."

I love winning.

11

The rest of our trip was uneventful. I kept expecting to see a wave of zombies come at us from the side of the road, but they only seemed to come in pairs. Brad ran them all down, waking Danny from his slumber every time.

Surprisingly, we didn't see any roadblocks or militia freaks or survivalists, either, which was a change from our original trip north. The remnants of the roadblocks were there, but they had all been busted. We stopped and checked a couple of them out with the floodlight, but they were stripped clean of bodies and anything useful.

They hadn't been overrun.

They had left.

"Where do you think they went?" Sean asked after the fourth abandoned roadblock.

"Not a clue," I said.

Brad just grunted.

I could feel the growing tension in him, in all of us. We had been up there on our island of a farm, and things had happened here. And we didn't know what.

We also stopped at a couple fuel stations, which became more numerous. The first tank we checked, our siphon wasn't long enough. It couldn't reach whatever fuel might have been remaining at the bottom of the tank. The tank may have been empty.

The second stop netted us a full tank of diesel, and a few full gas cans, too. We knew we had to stock up.

The creepy thing about getting the fuel—no zombies. Not one in sight the whole time we spent filling the tanks and ransacking the store for gas cans.

"Where did they all go?" Danny asked, having awoken from his slumber.

"South, I hope," Brad said. "Maybe they'll all eventually migrate south."

"Wishful thinking," I said, and wished I hadn't.

After that stop, it took about twenty minutes to get to the outskirts of Lynnwood, where we were greeted with the carnage of that first night. The bones of the buildings that had burned stood as shadows against the darkening sky where they managed to remain standing.

We saw zombies, now and then, milling about. Each time they saw us, they gave chase. We didn't shoot 'em, though, just tried to outrun them, or overrun them if they were in front of us.

Before we knew it, we were driving up the road to his father's house.

We passed Brad's old, beat up car, slowly. Sean whipped out the spotlight and played it over the car. It was trashed.

He then played it up the street towards Brad's father's place.

The street was essentially empty.

But piled against the fence, there had to be a hundred or more bodies. The dead. It didn't look much different from when we had stopped there three months ago to try to pick up his step-mom, just before his father died.

Nothing moved.

Brad drove the Humvee up to the fence. I readied my pistol. I heard Danny readying his rifle.

When we were ready, we waited.

Nothing emerged from the house.

"I wish the phones still worked," Brad said.

I wasn't relishing entering the house.

Apparently, neither was he.

12

We waited a few minutes more before we decided that a hundred zombies weren't going to rush out of the house and attack us as soon as we left the safety of the Humvee.

I got out, went to the gate. I had to climb over a pile of zombie bodies to do so. They squished and rolled underneath me. My boots, leather work boots I'd taken to wearing once I realized that three inch heels weren't conducive to surviving the zombie apocalypse, quickly picked up a sheen of gore that would require a thorough scrubbing before I would allow myself to get back into the Humvee—unless getting back in the Humvee meant survival and scrubbing my boots meant death.

After a little fiddling, I got the gate unlocked and pushed it open. Before it slid fully open, it caught on the arm of a long dead zombie, so rotted that it was impossible to tell whether it was man or woman. A good hard shove on the fence broke the arm from the torso, allowing the gate to open wide enough to fit the Humvee.

I jogged away from the gate as Brad drove up and over the pile. I didn't want to get splashed with three month old bodily fluids.

When the Humvee was through, I ran back to the gate, closed and locked it.

We were in. No turning back if a thousand zombies had chosen the house as a place to hang out. We'd never get the Humvee back through the gate without getting eaten alive.

Brad shut off the Humvee. No sense wasting the fuel.

Brad, Sean, and Danny all climbed out.

Each had their own flashlight. Thank god for LED flash-lights. We had replacement batteries, but we hadn't yet had to change the batteries in the flashlights.

"So, what now?" I asked.

"I guess we go in," he said, sounding disappointed.

To tell the truth, I was disappointed, too. Anyone in the house should have heard the Humvee. I expected to see *some* sort of movement, either zombies or people, but the place felt dead. Nothing moved. In one of those quirks of late fall weather, not even the air moved.

"We could wait for sunup," I said.

"Yeah," said Sean. "I don't want to go in there in the dark."

Brad looked up at the house and tapped his flashlight against his leg while flipping it on and off.

"You guys are right," he said without turning back to us. "It doesn't make any sense to go in now, but..."

I knew what was eating at him. His sense of duty. The same thing that had been eating at him for the last two months.

"Do you want to find out in the dark?" I asked him.

"There's no power," he said. "They barricaded themselves in the basement. It'll be dark down there no matter what."

"But in the morning..." Sean said.

Brad spun on him.

"Fuck! Are you listening to me? I promised her I would be back. I'm back. I know they're probably dead down there, but I have to find out! If you don't want to come, don't come. In fact, Sean, you stay here and keep Danny safe."

"Brad, I..."

"No. You're right. Your gimp ankle could be a liability down there, anyway. Stay here. Man the gun. Keep an eye out. This place is fucking creeping me out, but I have to know. I have to know."

His voice trailed off as he turned away and took his first steps toward the front door of the house.

I followed him. There was no question I would follow. I would never let him do this shit alone.

13

Brad put his hand to the brass doorknob of the front door. He had stowed his flashlight in his pocket. I had my flashlight in one hand, my gun in the other. A pair of spare clips were in my pocket. I hope I didn't have to use them. They held the last of my bullets.

"Ready for this?" he asked me.

"Yeah," I said.

"I love you, Andrea," he said.

"I love you, too," I said. "But don't forget your promise. You have to marry me."

"We need a pastor," he said.

"Have Sean do it. I mean, who is really going to go looking for our marriage certificates?"

"Can we quit stalling now?"

"You'll have Sean do it?"

"Yeah."

"Then open the door," I said. "What the fuck are you waiting for? We've got a ceremony to get to."

Brad chuckled. A good sign, considering the emotional outburst from just a couple minutes earlier.

Then he opened the door.

The reek that wafted out made me want to gag. From the way Brad turned his face away from the door, I gathered that he felt the need to spew bile, too.

Neither of us did, though. The reek wasn't especially unique, just strong.

"There's a lot of dead in here," he said after a cough.

"Yeah, and they had somehow kept the place shut up. You really think..."

He looked at me, and with that look, told me to shut up.

I know what a *need to know* is. It's what drove me out of my house as teenager. I needed to know, I stopped at nothing, and I found out too much when I opened the door to his safe one day and found a dozen big packages of cocaine and a bunch of other shit that I had no idea what it was.

My father, ex-military man, had turned to running drugs, and I ran from him as fast as I could. I had no desire to end up in the protection of CPS as a seventeen year old.

Need to know is dangerous.

Brad pulled his flashlight out, played it around the inside of the house.

Corpses littered the floor, most with bullet wounds to the head, others without heads at all.

"How many people were here?" I asked him.

"There were a lot of people here. I couldn't have counted them. It was chaotic. Probably most of the neighborhood."

And they all died in the house they thought would protect them.

Someone got in, infected them all.

Brad stepped through, holding his sword up.

I stepped in behind him.

One of the first things I noticed as I played my own flashlight around the walls and the windows was that none of the windows were broken, despite the hundreds of bullet holes in the walls.

"Did your dad put armored glass in the windows?" I asked.

"It wouldn't surprise me. He prepared everything to the extreme."

"So, where do we go?" I asked.

I tried not to breathe through my nose, but breathing through my mouth was almost worse. I could taste the decay in the air.

He stepped in the direction of a corridor, carefully avoiding the body of an older woman. The body was so decayed, I could only guess by the color of the hair and the clothing, a flower-print dress that looked like it had come right out of the seventies.

"This way," he said.

He lead me down that corridor toward the back of the house. Away from the entrance, the body count tapered off a little. The stench remained as strong as ever, but at least I didn't have to see the dead faces and the broken skulls quite so often.

You know how they say seeing this kind of thing desensitizes you? I was still sensitive. I knew I'd be having nightmares about it for weeks.

Brad lead me to a double door, pushed it open with the tip of his sword.

He played the flashlight into the room beyond.

Weapons covered the walls. A hundred of them. Maybe more. Rifles, swords, machine guns. A desk sat prominently in the middle of the room. It was clearly Brad's father's office, but the decorations.

His dad and my dad would have had something to talk about.

"Your dad didn't believe in gun safes, did he."

"No," Brad said. "His house was his safe. Do you need more ammo?"

"I could use some."

"The chest over there."

He pointed to an ornately decorated chest of drawers that stood about four feet tall.

I walked over to it, pulled open a drawer. It was filled to the top with ammunition, organized and labeled. A treasure trove.

But not what I needed at the moment.

I looked through several more drawers before I found what I needed. No extra clips, but three boxes of hollow point rounds. I stuff them in the pockets of my coat. No guaranteeing we'll be back, even though we planned to come back.

While I worked my way through the ammunition, Brad went to his father's desk and looked through it.

When I turned to see what he was doing, papers were flying out of the drawers at a rapid clip.

"What are you doing?"

"Looking for the key," he said.

"The key?"

"Yeah. There should be an extra key to the basement bunker in here."

I glanced over my shoulder at the doorway, making sure we were still alone.

"Maybe your step-mom took it," I said, turning back to him.

"She might have, but she should have had... Oh."

"What?"

Brad pulled a small, wooden box from the desk, no larger than a deck of cards. It had a falcon engraved on its lid.

"What is that?" I asked, as I walked over to get a better look.

Brad set it on the desk, then undid a small gold catch on the front and opened the lid.

Inside, snuggled together like lovers on a quilted red cushion, sat a pair of rings, gold, engraved with the same design that was on the top of the box. They looked like wedding rings. A man's ring, free of jewels, and a woman's ring with a single diamond—the prongs holding it looked like a falcon's talons.

"What are those?"

"My parents' wedding rings. I didn't know he kept them."

I wasn't quite sure what to say. He'd told me the story of how his parents came apart. Looking at the rings, and how his father had kept them, it was hard for me to believe his parents had ever split up.

Brad picked up the rings, held them together under the beam of his flashlight.

And then he put them right back into the box, closed and latched the lid, and stuffed the box into his pocket.

He went back to rooting through the desk.

I turned around again and watched the door. The house was too quiet for me. Every noise that Brad made in the desk caused me to flinch.

In between flinches, when I wasn't thinking about what might be coming to get us, I kept wondering what Brad intended to do with the rings. I had my hopes, but I couldn't mention them. I knew how he felt about his parents' divorce, and he had hated his father for it. But, that day, when they came to rescue me, it seemed they had reconciled.

And his father had kept the rings.

"Ah, here," he said.

I looked behind me.

He held up a key.

Which meant one thing, and I didn't like it very much.

Time to go down into the dark.

14

Brad lead me out of his father's office and down another hallway to a door.

The door stood open, exposing an empty stairwell.

I shined my light down the stairs.

Strangely, they were free of dead bodies, and free of zombies.

"Brad," I said. "This just isn't right. Where are all the zombies?"

"Maybe they left?"

He was just hoping. He had to be.

"They wouldn't just leave," I said.

"Why not?"

"If they just left, it means there's no one down there alive."

Brad shined his light up so he could see my face.

"I need to know," he said. "As soon as I know, we can leave. We can get our weapons, get ammo, get whatever else might be useful, and get the fuck out. But I have to..."

I put my hand up, silencing him.

"I know. Just get going. I don't think I can stand the stench much longer."

Brad took the first step down into the depths of his father's house.

I know it sounds crazy, but at that moment, I would have rather fought a zombie or six than take one step down those stairs. There was nothing good at the bottom. I knew it. His step-mom had said they had a month's worth of food. They could probably stretch it to six weeks, maybe eight. But three months was pushing it unless they started eating each other.

And I didn't think that was likely.

Not that I knew Brad's step-mom very well. Maybe she could be a cannibal.

But I followed Brad down those stairs, anyway.

At the bottom, there was a little foyer of sorts, a place to stand while they opened the door. A solid concrete wall blocked off the rest of the basement. A steel door was its only entrance, and it was sealed shut.

I shined the flashlight on the floor. Dried black blood coated the floor, but no bodies. If someone had died here, they had been dragged away, or they had walked away.

Brad tried the door.

It was locked shut.

He pulled out the key, stuck it in the lock, and twisted until we heard the click of the lock in the dead silence.

He pushed the door open and stepped through.

I could do nothing but follow with my flashlight in one hand, my gun, ready to shoot the first motherfucker that came at me, in the other.

Inside, the room looked well kept. Everything was in order. Chairs, couches, beds, all made up, straightened up, covered with plastic to protect them. Even the smell of the dead had hardly breached the walls.

Brad walked through the basement, flashing his light on everything, looking for something.

"Where did they go?" he asked.

I had no answer, but they were gone. It almost looked as if they had never been in here.

"She wouldn't have lied to you, would she?" I ask.

Brad looked up from the kitchen counter where he was running his hand across the counter-top.

"Lied?"

"Remember when we came by here that night? The lights were out. It looked empty then. She wouldn't have just run that night, would she?"

"Why would she? We were coming back. And she said there were too many..."

Brad's eyes shifted as he had a different thought.

"The blood," he said. "The blood on the floor outside the room. They were down here at one point."

I joined Brad in looking through the abandoned room. Maybe there was a clue somewhere. I ran my flashlight over every surface I could find, every wall, hoping to find a trace.

Brad gave up before I did.

"It's useless. They left. The cupboards are bare. They stayed here as long as they could, I think, but not long enough for me."

At least she wasn't dead. I think it would have really hurt Brad to discover he had failed her.

"She must have assumed something happened to us," I said.

I kept my flashlight moving.

I turned around.

My flashlight caught a slip of yellow.

I moved toward it.

It was a note on yellow legal paper, taped to the wall.

"Brad," I said. "Come see this."

He nearly ran across the room. Soon he was standing next to me, peering up at the note.

Brad,

Sorry you couldn't get here in time. I hope you are well. We're out of food. We haven't heard the zombies in days. On the radio, about three weeks ago, we heard there were refugee camps east of the mountains in Ellensburg and Wenatchee. We're going to make for the Ellensburg camp.

Please, if you made it back here, come look for us there. I know what you think of me, but I still consider you family, and I think your father would be terribly upset with me if I didn't try to look after you.

Alicia

She had dated it November thirteenth. Three days earlier.

15

Before we returned to the Humvee, I found a towel and did my best to wipe the gore from my boots. It wouldn't come off. I only gave them a more uniform coating of gore. I tried the water. It wasn't running, and I wasn't all that surprised.

Eventually, I gave up. I would have to leave them sitting outside the Humvee. I wasn't going to carry the stench inside with me.

Brad and I said little to each other when we got back to the Humvee. I could tell Brad wasn't ready for it. He'd prepared for every eventuality, I think, other than the one where his step-mother leaves him. It wasn't like it was his own mom, but she was the last family he had. Hell, if Brad would just follow through on his promise to marry me, she would be the last family *we* had. My dad, even if he was still alive, didn't count.

No. There was Danny, too. I was just going to adopt Danny for my own, no matter what anyone said. And there wasn't anyone to say different. Not even Brad would change my mind on that.

So we slept in the Humvee until the sun came up.

Over the hours that we slept, it grew colder outside. The windshield froze over, and our breath generated wisps of fog whenever we exhaled.

When I woke, Brad was already up in the cupola keeping watch. I pulled at his pant leg, and he came down.

"Take a look," he said.

I climbed up into the cupola to get a look around.

The landscape had frozen. Everything, from the trees to the bushes to the bars of the fence wore a layer of ice crystals. The clouds above hung in the sky, low and gray.

"You think it'll snow?" I asked.

"It's a good bet," he said.

"It'll make things hell in the mountains."

"Right."

I poked my head down inside the Humvee again, back where it was imperceptibly warmer.

"Danny, Sean. Wake up. We gotta get the shit we need and get moving."

"Huh? Why?" Sean asked as he struggled up from his shortened nap.

"If we're going to catch up with Alicia," Brad said, "we have to get moving. There might be snow in the forecast, and I don't wanna get fucked in the mountains."

I looked at Brad, raised my eyebrow.

"You don't?" I asked.

"Not what I meant," Brad said.

"Would you please leave that talk for when we're not around?" Sean asked.

"Sorry," I said.

But I wasn't.

I wasn't sorry at all.

We got out and got to work. Danny hung out in the cupola, watching for our zombie friends, who had remained curiously absent. The rest of us worked through the house, first ferrying weapons and ammo from Brad's father's office to the Humvee, then searching for other supplies.

We found ammo for the big gun on the Humvee in a safe in a locked vault in the garage. The same key that opened the basement opened that vault. We loaded the Humvee up with every round we could carry. We were going to Ellensburg, and we weren't likely to find any more.

We weren't likely to come back, either.

We didn't find any food in the house. Alicia and the two people she was with had either eaten it all or taken it with them. Because of the note, I suspected they had eaten everything while they waited for us to show up.

I did find a pair of boots to take. They weren't quite as comfortable as my old boots, but they didn't smell like rotting corpse, either.

It took us just about an hour to get everything together. We finished just as it started snowing.

Brad started up the Humvee, and I went for the fence.

I opened it, making sure not to step in anything putrid with my new boots, and then ran back to the Humvee and climbed in.

Brad looked at me, blinked a couple times, then shrugged.

"I guess there's really no reason to shut it behind us," he said.

"If you want it shut, you can do it. I'm not walking through dead bodies again."

He put it in gear and rolled us down the driveway and through the fence.

As we were pulling out, Sean said, "Look. To the left."

We looked.

A pair of zombies shambled out from between a couple of burned out houses.

The first we had seen since arriving the night before.

Somehow, the world seemed a little more normal as we drove past them. A lot less empty.

Brad drove us slowly across an overpass that spanned I-5. We hadn't been able to see much of anything the previous night, but as we crossed, the magnitude of what had happened became clear to us again.

I had forgotten.

Dead hulks of cars stretched as far as the eye could see in both directions. The falling snow obscured much of what we could see, but we should have been able to see downtown Lynnwood. It was gone, however. Only black skeleton fingers of a few buildings stuck up from the ground to remind us it had ever existed—the same fingers we had seen as shadows upon entering the night before.

"What's that?" Danny asked.

"Where?" I asked.

"On the left. To the..."

"To the north," Brad said, finishing Danny's sentence.

Movement. Between the cars. People walking, sliding between the cars like sand through separated fingers.

But not people.

"Zombies," Sean said under his breath.

Even over the rumble of the Humvee's engine, we all heard him.

"How many are there?" I asked.

Brad brought the Humvee to a stop, then reached down between us, pulled out the binoculars stowed there.

He looked through them for a few moments, then he handed them to me.

I leaned across him while I tried to get a look out his window.

It came clear as I held the binoculars to my eyes.

"Hundreds," I said.

They weren't running, just walking, but they were everywhere. Heading south along the freeway. Their numbers stirred visions of some sort of dark flood. I half expected the cars to begin to float with them.

"No," Brad said. "I think there are thousands."

I thought about telling him to shut up, but it wouldn't change the fact he was right, and I wouldn't have been able to get the words out through my quickly constricting throat.

Thousands of zombies.

I forced myself to breathe. My throat relaxed a little.

"Migrating," I said.

"Yeah," Brad said.

"What, like birds?" Sean asked.

"Not like birds," Brad said. "Like..."

"Like birds."

"What are we going to do?" Danny asked.

I handed the binoculars to Brad and sat back in my seat, then turned to look at Danny. He looked worried.

"We're going to drive away from here," Brad said. "We're going to drive and go over the mountains to somewhere they can't reach us."

He put his foot into the gas and drove us off that bridge and back to Highway 9.

"What *are* we going to do, Brad," I asked.

"We're going to have to refuel before we try to cross the mountains, otherwise, we won't have enough to make it, even with the full gas cans."

"Which means we have to get far enough ahead of that swarm in order to have time to fill the tank," I said.

We looked at each other then. Neither of us said it.

But Sean did.

"Aren't the roads going to get worse as we keep going south?"

"Shut up, Sean," I said. "We'll figure it out if that happens."

I didn't want to think about it.

The vision of thousands of zombies pouring south between the cars on the freeway was enough of a frightening thought.

17

Brad drove west along a thin, winding road, flanked on either side by tall fir trees and the occasional abandoned home. He wanted to get to Highway 9 as quickly as he could, and drove faster than I thought reasonable, weaving between stalled and abandoned cars, trying not to skid off the road in the accumulating snow. I held on to my seat.

Even so, I doubt we were making more than about 20 miles an hour, perhaps less. And as Sean so adroitly predicted, it only got worse as we drove.

"I think we should create a new calendar," I said to take my mind off the drive.

"A new calendar?" Sean asked.

"Yeah," I said. "We're now in Year One, PZA."

Brad glanced over at me. "Post Zombie Apocalypse?"

"Yup. I mean, after this, AD seems a tad outdated."

"So the year now begins, when? In August?"

"Yeah," I said, sitting up a little. "We probably need new names for the months, though."

"Like what?"

"I don't know. Braintober. Rotember."

"Dismember," Sean said.

"Oh my god," Brad said. "You have got to be kidding."

"Christmas would have to change, too," said Sean.

"Christmas?" Danny said, sounding more than a little worried that the holiday would change.

"Yeah," Sean said. "After all, since everyone rises from the dead, now, Jesus doesn't exactly have a corner on the market, any more."

"That's Easter, you freak," I said. "Don't worry, Danny. We won't change Christmas."

"What about the other holidays?" Brad said.

"Like what?" I asked.

"Independence day."

"Kind of pointless, now," said Sean.

"Halloween?"

I laughed. "Every day is Halloween, now."

"Without the candy," Danny said, sounding sullen.

"We'll find you some candy when we stop for gas," I said. "How's that?"

"Speaking of gas," Brad said, causing the whole mood to deflate, "what do you think about trying to get some soon?"

"How much is left in the tank?"

"About three quarters," he said.

"Why now?" I asked. "What are you thinking?"

"I was thinking that we would turn south toward Wood-inville once we reach Highway 9. But I'm thinking maybe we should just cross it and take back roads out to Fall City.

We have to get on I-90 at some point, and I'd prefer to do it as close to the mountains as possible. My worry is that there are fewer gas stations along the back roads, and possibly a higher chance of being empty."

Outside the Humvee, the snow fell steadily, but not real heavy. There was probably an inch or so on the ground.

"The roads will be worse on the back roads, won't they?" Sean asked.

"Only because of the weather," I said, though the likelihood of bandit traps would be greater.

"So what do you think?"

"Let's do it," I said.

Going south into the progressively larger towns on the east side of Lake Washington sounded like a recipe for disaster.

The next intersection turned out to be Highway 9, where we would have turned south. On the corner, there was a gas station and a mini-mart. Half a dozen abandoned cars sat in the parking lot and at the tanks. People must have been trying to get gas, and got zombied in the process.

Brad pulled in, Sean climbed up to the big gun.

We waited for a few moments, eying the place for evidence of the less than alive, and even the alive. Nothing moved but the falling snow.

I pulled an AR-15 from our new stash of weapons, loaded it, and exited the Humvee. Brad jumped out the other side, then walked around the front to meet me.

"With the snow, we're going to need a broom to find the tanks," I said.

"And you promised Danny some candy," Brad said.

"What was I thinking?"

"Inside?" he asked.

For an answer, I started walking toward the mini-mart part of the station. Brad followed behind me.

The glass of the station doors was long smashed. It crunched under our feet as we approached. Snow drifted up onto the sidewalk, but it hadn't blown in. It wasn't likely to, either, since there was little wind with it.

What little sunlight there was lit up the front of the store through the windows, but the light couldn't reach the back, leaving it dark and gloomy. A perfect place for someone, or something, to hide.

"Next time, remind me to tape my flashlight to the barrel of this thing," I said.

"We'll have to find some tape, then," Brad said.

He pulled out his own flashlight.

Together, we stepped through the glassless doors.

Most everything edible was already gone. No bags of potato chips, no loaves of bread—not that those would be worth eating—no beef jerky. The shelves were pretty picked over.

"Maybe there's a broom behind the counter."

The top of the counter was a mess. The cash register stood open, turned sideways. Someone had unloaded it, probably in the first moments of the disaster.

Behind the counter, the bald-headed body of a man lay on its back. The black mark of a bullet hole marred the left side of the forehead. A streak of long dried blood ran down into the hairline.

Brad spun around behind me, flashing his light into the recesses of the darkness.

"You hear something?" I asked. I brought my gun up,

pointed it to the back of the shop.

"I thought so," he said.

We waited, him with his sword raised and his flashlight moving slowly across every surface he could make it reach, me with my eye to the gun sight and my heart pounding in my chest.

One minute.

Two.

"It must have been nothing," he said. "Find the broom."

I looked over the counter again, but couldn't find a broom back there. Off to my left, in the gray area where the light started to fade out, I saw a closet door.

"Brad," I said, pointing. "The closet."

He shined his light on it.

It was shut, and the handle looked like it had a keyhole. Great.

I worked my way around the counter and over next to the dead guy.

"What are you doing?" Brad asked.

"Getting the keys," I said. "That door is probably locked."

I bent down next to the dead man.

It was cold enough in the store that it kept the stench of his bloated corpse down.

I searched his belt, first, hoping to Heaven that he had the keys on a ring or a line, but no luck. He had one of those shop-clerk vests on. I patted the pockets of that, next.

"Andrea, hurry up."

I looked up, but I couldn't see him.

"I'm going as fast as I can," I said.

I returned my focus to the corpse. He'd been a chubby man, probably a slime-ball in his early fifties. I mean, really, you can't get a better job than clerk at a mini-mart in your early fifties? But then, maybe he was the owner.

I decided to cut him some slack. After all, he was dead.

I patted his pants pockets, cringing, and I heard the jingle of keys.

To get at them, I had to put one leg over his body, straddling him. There was no way I was going to try moving him. I didn't want him to break open or anything. The idea of it made me shudder.

I wriggled my hand into the pocket, hooked a finger around the key ring, ignoring the soft give of the corpse flesh as best I could, and withdrew my prize.

A set of keys.

"I hope one of these is the right one," I said.

"Andrea, get out here," Brad said. It sounded urgent.

I stood up and saw what he was looking at.

She couldn't have been more than three when she died. She would have been cute, I think. Dark brown hair pulled back with a red bow that had somehow miraculously survived the last several months. One of her legs had gone missing at some point. She pulled herself along the floor with her hands, head up, watching us. She hungered, but could not move fast at all.

I was somewhat surprised that she hadn't eaten the man behind the counter, but maybe she had died after he did. I couldn't recall ever seeing the dead eat the dead.

"What do we do?" Brad asked.

He can be such a wuss sometimes.

I reached over and took his sword from him, handed him the AR-15, then walked the dozen feet between us and her and brought the blade down on her head, ending her second life. I didn't want to waste a bullet.

"You never fail to surprise me," Brad said as I handed him his sword. He didn't quite look all right. We hadn't seen too many child zombies, but every one we did see made him indecisive. Of the two of us, you probably would have thought I would be the one to be squeamish about killing zombie children, but they looked to me like tiny little monsters. There was nothing human left in them.

Brad, though, couldn't seem to get past what they used to be. I worried that he'd eventually come across one that didn't look quite so dead, and he would get too close in order to try to save it which would result in him losing his life to a three year old.

I loved kids, but the dead are dead.

"She was already dead, Hun," I said. "I don't want her making us dead."

I took my weapon back from him, then walked to the closet door and tried the handle.

It opened.

"Fuck!" I said.

"What?"

I threw the keys at him. "See if these do anything useful. The door was unlocked."

That brought some nervous laughter at my expense.

Inside the closet, a broom, a mop, and a pile of other useless sundries.

I took the broom.

And then I caught myself looking around, and my eyes came to rest on the body of the dead girl. Suddenly, the air didn't feel quite right. I grew conscious of how much time we were wasting.

"Grab Danny his candy and let's get out of here," I said. I could feel the clock ticking.

18

It took us a few minutes, using the broom, to find the opening to the underground tank holding the gold that would power our chariot, minutes that seemed to drag on as we raced across the parking lot dragging the broom behind us.

Danny sat in the cupola munching on gummy bears Brad had found. He had a smile on his face, but he had his eyes out on the world around us, searching for the enemy.

When we finally found the cover, a crowbar and Brad's muscles pried it open. Sean backed the Humvee up to the tank, while Brad slipped our siphon hose down as far as he could. The cool thing about the hose was the hand pump that worked with it. We could pump whatever we wanted out of the tank without drowning ourselves in fuel.

"I count our blessings every time we need to fuel that this thing takes diesel," Brad said while he cranked away at the hand pump.

We all did. All the regular gas had been emptied from most of the stations within the first few hours after the zombies appeared. The diesel, though, most people ignored it. There was usually something left, though it hadn't been that way up north. All the farmers had gone and filled their dump trucks and whatever other equipment they had, which is why we had run out up there.

But the tank beneath our feet at that moment was near full.

"You were cursing it at the farm," I said.

"I know. But down here..."

"Zombie!"

Danny's shout caused Brad and I to look up. Brad stopped pumping. The zombie was on the other side of the Humvee. Neither Brad, nor I, could see it.

"Pump," I said. "I'll take care of it."

He started cranking again, but faster. The problem with the hand pump—it took more time.

I walked around the front of the Humvee, trying to keep my balance in the snow, which was starting to pile up. Two inches, at least. Elsewhere, that's not saying much, but in and around Seattle, it's dangerous.

I didn't see the zombie at first.

"Where?" I asked.

"North, up the highway," said Danny.

I had to squint to see through the snow.

And then I saw it. A lone figure walking down the center of the road, its gait severely off center. It had disappeared for a moment behind a dark blue van that had skidded off the road and overturned.

Four hundred yards, maybe.

I lifted the gun, put my eye to the sight.

Pulled the trigger.

And walked a trio of bullets from his chest to his forehead. The last one was the one that put the thing into the snow, hopefully never to get up. The sound of the rifle echoed amongst the trees and the hills that surrounded us.

I stood in the snow, watching.

Waiting.

The clock running in my head.

The snow still falling.

The click-click-click of the hand pump running full speed behind me.

"There's another," Danny said.

His eyes were sharper than mine. I couldn't pick it out through the snow at first.

But after a moment, I saw it.

He was right.

Another one.

"There's two of them," Danny said.

"Fuck," said Sean.

Yeah. Fuck is right.

"Brad! Pack it up!" I yelled.

The first zombie broke into a run.

I sighted, pulled the trigger. It went down.

The other one started running, too.

"Brad!"

"I'm working on it!"

He had to let the fuel drain out of the siphon. Close the cap. Thirty seconds or so.

I backed up against the Humvee so that I'd be close to a door, then put the other zombie in my sight and shot it dead.

Crap, crap, crap.

"How are they so close?" I asked.

"I don't know," Sean said. "Maybe they're ahead of the ones on the freeway."

Three more appeared out of the fog of snow.

I heard the door on the other side of the Humvee open.

"Brad's getting in, Andrea," Sean said.

I pulled open my door.

The zombies ran. Three hundred yards.

"Start the fucker up," Brad said.

The Humvee rumbled to life.

It was facing the wrong way, though.

I climbed in and shut the door. Through the window, the zombies had closed the gap even more. Two hundred yards. Behind the lead zombies, another twenty. Thirty.

"Get us out of here, Sean!"

"Should I shoot 'em?" Danny asked.

"Not yet," I said. "Save the ammo."

Sean put the Humvee into reverse, backed through the parking lot, narrowly avoiding an abandoned red Honda. He backed around the side of the building, and that gave us good access to Highway 9.

That's not where we wanted to go, though.

A hundred yards between us and the zombies.

"Danny, get down here."

I wished Brad was driving, but there was no time to switch drivers. Gunners, though.

Danny climbed down without questioning me, and up I went.

The snow was coming down, cold. I knew being up there would be lousy, and it wasn't likely to get better, but I was the best shot we had.

"No, no, go out the other way," said Brad. I could hear him talking to Sean, but I couldn't hear Sean's responses.

The tires spun in the snow just a bit as Sean drove us forward, past the red Honda, then out onto Highway 9, heading north.

What the hell was he thinking? We wanted to go east, didn't we?

Time to start shooting.

I swung the gun around until I had the lead zombie in sight. Pulled the trigger.

The first round obliterated its chest. The head fell off, because there was nothing left for it to attach to.

On to the next one.

They were no more than fifty yards away.

Sean put his foot into the gas, burning it away as the tires spun. Fuck. We just went to all that effort to get more fuel and Sean was going to waste it.

I heard Brad yelling, but couldn't make it out.

I pulled the trigger.

It took three bullets to take down the zombie that I aimed at, though another zombie behind it took a round in the shoulder. The only benefit to having so many zombies in one place.

The tires caught and we jerked forward.

The zombies started to enter the intersection. We had twenty feet ahead of us before we could turn.

More shots, more zombies fell. It wouldn't be enough.

Closer, closer. The zombies to us, us to the intersection. They filled the far half. More than thirty, now. A hundred.

Blam, blam, blam.

I didn't stop firing, but I tried to make each shot count. Get the ones in the front.

The front of the Humvee entered the intersection, and Sean spun the wheel to the right, hard.

The lurch caused me to miss a shot

The zombies were right below me. I kept shooting, but I couldn't hit the closest ones.

The rear of the Humvee slipped out, smashed into the wall of zombies, knocking a half dozen of them over. The skid stopped as the tires caught on a zombie body.

A zombie reached out, caught the rear ladder of the Humvee.

I reached for the machete that we kept up there ever since Brad's father got bit.

I waited, not shooting.

The Humvee raced clear of the zombie wall, leaving them trailing behind us.

The one climbing the ladder looked up at me. He had a name tag on. Bill Hughey, Account Manager, First Island bank. I blinked, amazed I had managed to read that.

Bill's left hand reached for the top rung, grabbed it.

I waited.

I wanted the fucker dead, not dismembered.

I chuckled at the memory of our new calendar month.

His right hand came up, bringing his head within reach.

I shouted. His dead crazed eyes looked into mine for a half second.

I brought the machete down on his skull, cleaving it in half, all the way down to the top of the spine.

Bill lost his grip.

He tumbled backward off the Humvee, leaving a streak

of blood and brains on the ladder.

"You all right?" Brad shouted up from inside.

I looked up. The zombies were behind us. Some were trying to follow, but most were continuing through the intersection.

Crazy.

Maybe they weren't really hungry. Maybe they were migrating. Like birds.

"Yeah," I said. "I'm all right. We just had a passenger I needed to cut loose."

19

With Sean driving, I took the opportunity to climb down from the turret so that I could sit next to Brad and hold him for a moment.

Danny took one look at us, pulled his hood over his head, tightened it around his ears, and climbed up into the turret.

I put my arm around Brad, and he hugged me tight. I would have preferred it if we had been able to do that with far fewer clothes on, but I would take what I could get. I wasn't going to be picky and demanding when, at any moment, a horde of zombies could emerge from the forest to swallow us up.

"Brad," I said. "What if the zombies reach Fall City before we get there?"

"They won't get there before we do," he said, trying, but failing, to be reassuring.

"What makes you so sure? We're driving east, across their front. They're moving closer to us all the time."

"I'm hoping that they're only following the easiest routes," he said. "The highways, freeways. The path of least resistance."

"And if they're not?"

"Then we're fucked," he said.

"Brad..."

"Look, sorry. Fall City is still south of us. We're still traveling south and east, just not as quickly. We're driving. We'll beat them."

Apparently, I didn't look convinced. It's not that I was afraid, but dammit, I was beginning to wonder. The horde seemed to be getting closer and closer.

"Look, we're going to head out Paradise Lake road, then take Woodinville Duvall road into Duvall, then take 203 south to Fall City. Getting to any of those roads from the north is difficult. Highway 9 is the only road that leads north from any of them, and we're off that, now."

It made sense as he said it.

I could only hope he was right about the path of least resistance. I couldn't help but glance out the window at the world of snow covered trees off to our left and wonder.

My wondering led me to thinking about Randy and his family.

"Do you think Randy escaped them?" I asked.

Brad was slow to answer. I wondered if he felt guilty about what we did to them, but I wasn't going to ask. I didn't feel guilty at all. Just curious.

"I'm sure they escaped," Brad said eventually. He brought his hand up to brush my hair back. "We didn't leave them with nothing, and they've had just as much time to get south of there as we did. And I'm sure they didn't head to Lynnwood and spend the night. They're probably ahead of us, perhaps even across the pass already."

"I still don't believe they weren't going to tell us," I said.

"The world has changed," Brad said.

I kissed his bearded face. His whiskers tickled my cheeks, but I didn't care. I was getting used to it, and it kept him warm. After I was done, I leaned back in his arms.

"Do you mind if I take a nap?" I asked.

His arms tightened around me protectively.

"Go right ahead," he said.

20

I couldn't sleep. Visions of the zombie horde ran through my head, again and again. I pretended to sleep, though. I wanted Brad to feel like he was comforting me.

So when the Humvee came to a stop, I had little idea where we were.

"What's up," Brad asked Sean.

"Look," Sean said, "off in the ditch."

I sat up. Looked.

Holy shit.

"I recognize that bus," Brad said.

"Yeah. Randy's bus," I said.

Randy's prison bus lay on its side, just off the road. They must have hit a patch of ice and slid off the road. Only a light dusting of snow covered the bus. The crash hadn't happened long ago.

"Where are we?"

"On 203, about three miles south of Duvall."

So they made it to 203 and through the tiny town of Duvall, at least. Brad hadn't been wrong about that.

"You see anyone, Danny?" Brad asked.

"No," Danny said.

"We've got to get out and look," I said.

Brad looked at me like I was crazy. "What? They were going to leave us behind."

"We should at least look," I said. "What about those kids? When the horde comes through..."

The thought of that little girl in the gas station ran through my head. The way Brad looked at me, I had a feeling he was replaying the same memory.

"The kids," he said.

I grabbed my rifle, shoved an extra magazine in my pocket, to go with the clips for my pistol, and flung open the door.

I crawled over Brad and jumped out into four inches of snow.

Shit. We didn't have much time. The roads into Fall City were going to be hell, even if they weren't blocked by abandoned cars.

Brad jumped out after me.

Together, we walked to the bus.

The bus lay with the driver's side up, burying the door in the snow and mud of the ditch. It had an emergency exit door in the back, but it was locked.

I slid down into the ditch, then banged on the door. Brad remained standing at the top.

"Hello!" I called out.

"Help!" It was a small voice, barely made it out of the bus.

"That sounds like the little girl," Brad said.

"Can you unlock the back door?" I shouted.

"No, it's blocked!" said the girl. I couldn't remember what her name was.

"They had all their shit in the back of the bus," Brad said. "I bet it's tumbled all over the place."

I crawled up out of the ditch, then walked along the length of the bus.

"Damn all the armored windows on this thing," I said.

"They keep zombies out," Brad said, walking along with me.

"Yeah, but they might end up killing everyone in the bus."

When we reached the front of the bus, I slid down into the ditch again and looked through the windshield.

I took a step back.

The windshield was cracked, and Derrick's mop of a head had caused the crack. The crash had tossed him face first into the windshield. His face had slid down the windshield, leaving a smear of blood behind it. He wasn't moving.

I fished my flashlight out of my pocket and shined it inside.

Everything was tossed about. Containers of fuel, pots, pans, clothing, whatever else they were carrying. There were limbs, here and there, sticking up from the seats.

I expected at least some of them to move, but for a moment, nothing did.

And then I saw her. The little girl pulled herself up against a seat. She was crying. The sound of her cry didn't make it out through the armor, but my flashlight lit up the tears that were coming down her face, mixing with blood from a gash on her head.

I kicked at the windshield with my boot, but that wasn't going to work.

"Brad, the hammer?"

"Right."

He ran off to get the sledge-hammer that we had stowed in the Humvee. It wasn't a full size one, there wasn't really enough room for that, but it would work wonders for driving tent stakes, if we ever thought it safe enough to sleep in a tent, and it would work for this.

"Stay calm, honey," I yelled to her. "We'll get you out."

She nodded. I don't know how she was hearing me if I couldn't hear her cries.

Brad returned with the hammer, slid down the embankment, and swung away at the windshield.

It took a dozen or more blows, but eventually, he broke the glass and made a hole big enough for us to climb through.

It was hard, getting back to her. I had to climb over all the detritus of the family. Brad came in behind me. He checked on each one of Randy's family as he went. I passed them all by, my eyes locked on the little girl, frightened, hurt.

"Are you hurt?" I asked her as I stepped over a large fuel can. The smell of diesel in the bus was strong. Some of them had opened.

"Yeah," she said, between sniffs.

"Where?"

"My leg," she said.

She was holding on to the back of a seat. I guessed the leg was broken or something.

I climbed over Grandma. She was dead, her neck bent

at an awkward angle up against the back of a seat. Weren't any of them wearing seat belts?

I saw Randy, too, inadvertently. I thought I saw him breathe, but I had to make the girl feel safe, first. I had to get her out of here. I couldn't let her become like that girl in the gas station. With her hurt leg, the similarities were all too many.

"What was your name, honey? I seem to have forgotten."

"Katrina," she said.

And then I surmounted one last obstacle in the form of a broken open steamer trunk and made it to the seat right in front of her, standing on the wall of the bus.

"Can you step around the seat?" I asked.

"No," she said. "It hurts."

I looked over the seat, and wished I hadn't.

Her leg had twisted at an ugly angle. That she was even holding herself up was an amazing feat.

I scooted around the seat, and bent down to look at the leg. I couldn't tell what was wrong. Her knee was either out of joint, or broken. Either way, she wasn't walking on it.

"Okay," I said. "Come here, and I'll carry you out."

"What about Andrew?"

"Andrew?" I asked.

"Yeah," she said.

"Who's Andrew?"

"My brother," she said.

Right.

"Do you know where he is?" I asked.

"He was sitting right in front of me," she said.

I glance to the seat I had just come from, over the top of the steamer trunk.

Oh shit.

Oh fuck.

I looked up, away from the sight. I didn't want to see it. Instead, I saw Brad crawling over a seat about halfway to me.

"Brad! I need your help! Her leg's broken, or worse," I said.

He gave up checking on people and came toward me as fast as he could.

"What about my brother?" Katrina asked.

"We'll help him if we can," I said.

"You can't, can you," she said. Her eyes bored straight into mine, daring me to lie to her. "I saw the trunk fall."

"No," I said. "I don't think I can. But we'll try."

She closed her eyes.

"Everyone dies, these days," she said. "Will he come back?"

As a zombie. Fuck.

"I don't think so, honey."

Brad reached us.

Katrina only screamed once as we picked her up and carried her out of the bus, despite all the bumps we gave her.

When we got her out of the bus, Brad called Sean over to help get her up the hill.

The two of them carried her up.

"I'm going back in," I said.

"Be careful," Brad said. "I smelled a lot of spilled fuel."

"I know. But I've got to check on her brother."

I had to be sure. Maybe, somehow, he survived.

My second trip to the back of the bus took less time. I could watch where I was going, and I didn't have to keep my eye on the little girl.

And when I got to Randy, I saw that he *was* breathing. I hadn't imagined it.

I reached down to him. He was crushed between two seats, blood flowing from the side of his head.

"Randy," I said. "Randy, can you hear me?"

One eye fluttered open.

"You," he said. His voice was phlegmy, like he had liquid in his lungs.

"Can you take my hand?" I asked.

"I killed them all," he said.

"No, no. You didn't kill them," I said. "It was an accident."

"No. I pushed him to drive faster. They're so close, now. I could feel them. They were following us. It's my fault they're dead."

"Katrina's not dead," I said. "Give me your hand. I'll help you out of here."

"You saved Katrina?" he asked.

"Yeah," I said.

"Even after..." he started coughing, but I knew what he meant.

"Yes. We stopped, even though we knew it was you."

"Your boyfriend, he didn't stop."

"I made him."

Randy's lip curled in what looked like an attempt to smile. Blood dribbled out of the corner of his mouth.

"What about Andrew? Is he..."

I took a breath as deep as I could, inhaling the diesel fumes. I couldn't stay much longer, and Randy wouldn't live much longer.

"He's fine," I said. "We brought him out, too."

Randy would never know the difference.

A gunshot rang out. It was the big gun on the Humvee.

"Andrea!" Brad's shout filtered down through one of the open windows.

I looked at Randy, and he looked at me. The old professor's one working eye told me he knew what that meant.

"Don't let them get me," he said.

"I won't," I said.

"You'll take care of them?" he asked.

"Of course."

I pulled out my pistol, pointed it at his head.

"No, no," he said. "the fumes. Use a knife, through my eye."

Into the brain.

Guaranteed dead.

The gun went off again. I didn't have much time.

I drew my knife, held it right below his eye.

"I'm sorry," I said.

"It's not your fault."

I stabbed the knife through the eye. Blood erupted out of it, and the last shred of Randy's life left him.

21

The gun spewed forth a half-dozen, a dozen, and then even more rounds, their reports echoing through the bus.

"Andrea, get the fuck out of there!" Brad shouted, almost hysterical.

With the damned windows all sealed, I couldn't see out of the bus, but the gun had fired too many rounds already for it to be anything good.

I left Randy lying there and scrambled back to the front of the bus. It wasn't easy, but I was getting better at it, except for when my boot slipped and came down on Grandma's head. I cringed as it shifted under me, but the continuing fire from the big gun left me no time to apologize.

I tripped going out the hole we had made in the windshield and rolled out into the ditch. My face ended up buried in the snow and the muck underneath that had only barley frozen.

Wham, wham.

Fuck.

I pushed myself up out of the muck and snow, wiped the snow off my face and spat out the mud that had seeped past my lips, then scrambled up the side of the ditch.

I looked to the north, past the bus, past the Humvee which was rolling up with its side door open to where I had exited the bus. All I could see was a wall of zombies flooding down the highway.

"Get in!" Sean yelled from his perch on top of the Humvee.

I dropped the rifle on the ground, left it behind. I had no time to carry it. I scrambled for the door, my feet slipping in the snow.

Somehow, I managed to stay upright enough to make progress.

But the zombies closed in on us faster than I could move.

Running. They had the scent of us.

I caught the door just as the first one, a particularly ugly one with a huge chunk missing from the side of its head, reached the rear of the Humvee.

Sean shot everything he could, but he couldn't get the close ones.

I pulled myself in by the door, grabbed the seat.

The zombies surged forward.

Something grabbed my foot as it hung out the door.

"Go! Go!" I said.

I felt, through the seat, the motor of the Humvee rev to life. We surged forward, the door banged against my shin, and whichever dead creep had ahold of me only strengthened its grip. It held on.

I tried to kick at the hand—I hoped it was a hand—that had grabbed my foot, but it wouldn't let loose.

I looked up and saw Danny. He had his gun out.

"Shoot it!"

I trusted him.

I had to.

My fingers were losing their purchase on the seat, and my new boot wouldn't come off. I would have given it up. I didn't like it that much.

A hand, its fingers strong as anyone alive, grasped onto my leg. It was pulling itself up.

"Shoot, Danny!"

Danny leaned over me. I couldn't see what he was doing, but I hoped he was taking careful aim. I didn't want a bullet in my leg.

"Hold still," he said.

I stopped kicking, but I was still dragging the zombie along, which caused my leg to bounce all over the place.

My left hand slipped, leaving me holding on by only my right.

The shot rang out through the cabin of the Humvee, and I cringed, unable to cover my ears.

The hands fell away from my leg.

I still had my boot.

Danny helped pull me in, and then I shut the door.

Brad looked over his shoulder at me while I sat in the seat trying to catch my breath.

"You bit?" he asked.

"No," I said.

"What took you so long in there?" he asked.

"I had to do a friend a favor."

I looked down at my hand.

For the first time, I noticed it was covered in blood. Randy's blood.

Whatever he was before, I'd call him friend forever.

22

Fall City was a ghost town when we drove through. The snow had stopped falling for the moment, but everything was blanketed in white—the burnt out buildings, the abandoned cars, the corpses. A lone, scrawny black lab wandered down the left side of the main street. It didn't look like it had fed in a while.

We passed gas stations, but the knowledge of the zombie horde behind us kept us pushing on.

Katrina sat up front with Brad, silent as anything. She hadn't said a word since we left the bus behind. I tried to get her to break her silence, but nothing I said seemed to penetrate.

We continued on from Fall City toward North Bend.

The trip up 202, where it winds around some pretty steep terrain, was harrowing—I kept expecting us to slide off the road in the snow—but Brad proved adept at navigating the hill.

At the top, he pulled into an empty parking lot marked by a sign that said *Snoqualmie Falls*, and told us all to get out.

"What are we doing?" I asked.

"When I was a kid," he said, "every time we drove this way, my father would make us get out and we would watch the water flow over the falls. Now get out."

When I was out, I could hear the roar of the water as it crashed down the falls.

Through a half a foot of snow, he forced us to trudge toward the observation area. He carried Katrina in his arms the whole way, taking care not to jostle her leg too much.

I had always seen the falls on postcards and crap. An icon of the Northwest. But I had never seen them up close.

The river ran pretty heavy. The water turned white as it fell over the edge in a never ending cascade. The roar was intense. I could barely hear myself think.

I looked over at Brad and Katrina. She watched the falls. He watched her. She turned her head, looked into his eyes, then said something into his ear. He said something back. I couldn't hear what either of them said over the din of the crashing water, but when the exchange was over, Katrina had a small smile on her face. It was amazing how resilient she was. But then, you were either resilient, or you went mad, or you died. There weren't any other choices.

After a couple minutes, I leaned over to Brad.

"The zombies?" I asked.

He frowned at me. I was ruining his moment, cutting short his memories.

"I guess you're right," he said.

We made our way back to the Humvee and climbed in.

I tried to take the seat up front, but Katrina looked at me with her big hazel eyes. "Can I sit up here, please?"

I couldn't say no.

North Bend was just as abandoned as Snoqualmie and Fall City. We had to detour around an abandoned ladder truck which, apparently, had been placed across main street as a wall. It didn't appear to have done any good. When we reached the other side, there was nothing but a pile of dead bodies eight feet high.

We found a gas station, filled up. We didn't go inside, though. We knew our time was short. With our stop at the falls, the zombie horde could be coming up the street at any moment.

Not long after, we found ourselves on I-90, heading east.

The freeway had a lot fewer cars than expected, but thinking back to what Lynnwood looked like, maybe none of the people in the metropolitan areas made it out.

The roadway proved more and more treacherous as we went. The snow piled higher with each passing mile, but

Brad pushed on, despite voicing concerns that we might not reach the top.

It started to get dark out, as well. Maybe five o'clock. Hard to tell without working cell phones or a watch.

I started to wonder about his step-mom. We didn't know how she was traveling, we didn't know what the weather had been like. We only knew she had left and her intended destination.

"You think she made it?" I asked Brad.

"I have to think so," he said, catching immediately that I was talking about his step-mom.

"What if there aren't any refugee camps?"

He looked at me.

"Are you going to be negative for the rest of the trip?"

"No," I said.

"She's there," he said. "There's a camp. There has to be."

For the next few minutes, I kept my eye on him, and wondered what his insistence meant. What if there wasn't? Would he break? Would he give up?

He'd had to watch his mom and his dad die. He had killed his dad, even though that had happened after his dad had died the first time.

He had looked peaceful while holding Katrina. The whole trip to the waterfall, incidentally, had reminded me that there were still beautiful things in the world. And the smile on Katrina's face, small though it was, had been a balm to my soul, though I had not known I needed it.

We saved her.

We got her out of that bus.

If we hadn't, she'd be wandering around dragging her leg behind her, looking for food in all the wrong places.

I had thought it was Brad that was affected by the little girl in the gas station.

But it was me.

Brad hit the breaks.

The wheels under the Humvee broke loose and we started to slide.

"Brad!" I screamed.

I wasn't the only one screaming.

In front of us, a dark wall loomed, blocking the freeway, and we were skidding toward it.

Brad let off the breaks, regained some control, and then pumped them, trying to slow us down, trying to keep us from crashing into it.

Then our tire hit something, and the Humvee spun sideways, completely out of control, still sliding toward that wall.

The back of the Humvee hit first. The sound of crunching metal assaulted my ears right as the side of the Humvee followed through, tossing all of us sideways.

I crashed into Sean, flew over him, and landed on top of Danny. He cried underneath me. He'd hurt something. My shoulder had hit the side glass, which, being armored, hurt my shoulder more than the glass.

The engine died.

All I could hear were Danny's cries, the moans of the rest of us, and the wind as it blew through the open cupola.

I extricated myself, got back to my seat, which allowed Sean to pull himself off of Danny.

"You all right, Danny?" I asked.

"My arm hurts," he said.

I reached into the pocket of my coat, pulled out my

flashlight and shone it on him. It was bright in the darkness beneath the wall, but I couldn't get a good look at Danny.

"Sean," I said.

"Right."

He took the flashlight from me, and used it to examine Danny.

"What the hell is a wall doing here?" Brad said.

So he was okay.

"Katrina, you okay?"

"Yeah," came her voice, but it was unsteady.

I could imagine.

Two wrecks in one day.

Fortunately, we were not dead.

But the cold was already starting to seep through the open cupola. We'd freeze to death if we didn't get going soon.

"Brad, we need to get moving," I said.

"I know," he said. "I'm trying to start it."

The cold couldn't have stopped it dead so quick, could it?

"Danny's fine," said Sean, handing me my flashlight back. "Bruised arm, I think."

Good.

It amazed me that we were all okay. If Brad had been driving any faster...

I let that thought go. It didn't matter.

"What's wrong," I asked. "Won't it start?"

"No. I don't know."

Fuck.

"I'm going out," I said.

"What?"

"While you try to get this thing started, I'm going to check out this wall, see if there's a way around it."

He grunted, tried the starter again. I heard it click, click, click, then nothing.

Fuck.

If the zombies came up the mountainside that far, we were dead. If we didn't find shelter, we were dead. If the people that had put up the wall weren't friendly...

I zipped up my coat, pulled the hood over my head, opened my door, and stepped out into a foot of snow.

First snowfall of the year, then, or earlier falls had melted off somewhat.

We were lucky.

Without snowplows, we could have been trying to walk through three or four feet of snow.

I ran my flashlight over the wall.

It was probably fifteen feet high, at least. Twenty. Made of logs.

"Hello!" I shouted into the twilight.

The only answer I got back was a blast of wind.

I walked the length of the wall, step by step, looking for a way through. Whoever made it had to have put a door in it.

I couldn't find one, though.

I found something else odd, too. There weren't any cars, no abandoned vehicles. Just us. If someone had blocked this to prevent people from getting through, I would have expected to see dozens of cars piled up.

I got to the edge of the road.

A guard rail, topped with snow, kept me from going any further.

A good thing, too. The other side of the rail led to a steep drop a hundred-fifty feet down.

I shined the light down, and it glinted off a piece of metal.

Cars.

A hundred of them. More, maybe.

I walked back to the Humvee, my feet frozen.

I thought I'd check to see if Brad had come close to getting it started again, but when I opened the door to ask, Katrina was there, looking at me, a tear in her eye.

"What's wrong, honey?" I asked.

"My leg hurts," she said.

I flashed the light down to look at her leg.

Her pant leg was covered in blood.

"Brad!"

"What?"

"She's bleeding! We don't stop this..."

Brad went for his belt.

I pulled out my knife and cut her pants open.

It was obvious why she was bleeding.

Her leg had been broken.

In the second crash, the bone was shoved through her skin, exposed.

I couldn't look.

"I've got this," Brad said. "You go see if you can find some help. There's got to be someone nearby."

Right.

"Help!" I called out.

Probably not smart.

"Help!"

I couldn't think of much else, though.

I went around the Humvee to walk the rest of the barrier.

"Help! We've got a little girl that's dying!"

Only my voice came back to me. That and a scream from Katrina.

And the wall was solid, implacable. It buttressed up against a stone cliff that was unscalable without climbing gear.

Katrina would die, and then we would all die before the night was through, unless we could find shelter and a fire.

Fire.

I ran back to the Humvee as fast as the snow and my boots would let me.

When I got there, Brad had put a tourniquet on her leg, and had shoved the bone back in and wrapped it up. He probably risked killing her doing that, but we didn't have much choice.

"We need to move the Humvee away from the wall," I said.

"Why?" Brad asked.

"We're all going to die out here unless we do something. We won't survive the cold."

"What are you thinking?"

I pointed to the diesel containers.

"The wall is made of wood," I said.

"Diesel can be hard to get burning," Sean said. "It's not like gasoline."

"Got a better idea?"

"No," he said.

He reached behind him, grabbed a can, and handed it to me.

Then he and Brad got out and struggled to push the Humvee away from the wall. It was slow going at first. They had trouble getting traction, but once it started, the downhill slope aided them.

It still didn't roll very fast. The snow kept it from gaining too much speed.

I opened the can and poured it over the section of the wall where we had it. Splinters stuck out from the wood. I made sure they were covered. They'd be a perfect place to get the fire started.

"We may not get through, tonight," I muttered as I splashed the diesel over the wood, "but at least we'll be warm."

"Hey, what are you doing?"

A man's voice from above, loud, but trying to be soft.

I looked up at him.

"Lighting this fucker on fire," I said.

I dropped the can, though. There was enough on the wood that it should help get it going.

"I wouldn't do that," he said.

"Then help us over this wall. We've got a little girl with a severely broken leg."

"I can't do that. Not at night. Go wait in your truck until morning, and we'll take a look, then."

"She'll be dead by then," I said.

I fished my flashlight out of my pocket, turned it on, and shined it up above.

A dark face hung out over the wall.

"Shut that off!" he said.

I wasn't about to. I caught the barrel of a rifle over his shoulder. If I could keep him from seeing me, all the better.

"Let us in," I said.

"I can't," he said. "There won't be no one here 'til morning."

"What kind of sanctuary are you running, if you won't

take in people that need help?"

"Sanctuary? This ain't no sanctuary. This is the front line. You're on the border between the dead and the living. Go to your truck, get in, hang tight 'til morning."

I started walking away.

"Can't do that," I muttered.

I walked the twenty feet back to where they had stopped the Humvee.

"They won't let us in," I said as I climbed in to the back seat. "Spouted some crap as to how we're on the front line between the living and the dead."

"Was he armed?" Brad asked.

"Yeah, but he didn't pull it off his shoulder. I'm not sure how many bullets he's got on him."

"Probably not enough," Sean said.

"So what now?" Brad asked.

"Try that engine again," I said. "See if we can get this running, keep us warm, make it look like we're going to play nice."

Brad smiled at me.

"And then set that wall to burn?"

"Yeah. It might be the time for one of those grenades you took from your dad's. That ought to light the diesel."

"Probably not," said Sean, "unless they're incendiary."

"Don't think so," said Brad.

"Start this thing up," I said. "I can't think in the cold."

"All right," he said.

He pushed the ignition one more time, and the thing turned over once, twice, then caught. It was rough for a moment, then started going.

The light came on.

A shadow moved just at the edge of the light.

"Shit," Brad said. "We're not alone."

Sean turned around, rifled through our mishmash of crap behind us.

I went up, took control of the big gun.

I turned on the spotlight.

The eyes of the dead lit up.

A dozen of them.

"Did they follow us?" I asked, not expecting an answer.

I sighted on the first, with the spotlight illuminating him.

Wham.

It fell over.

The second.

Wham.

Dead.

The third was an older lady who looked like she should have been dead long before she became a zombie.

Wham.

That round took out her and the one behind her.

I heard the right side door open. Sean climbed out into the snow. I looked down. He was carrying something, but in the dark, I couldn't see what.

"What the hell?" said the man atop his wall.

I ignored him, ignored Sean, and went back to shooting zombies.

Wham.

Wham.

I heard the pop of a flare gun.

Everything behind me lit up for a moment, and then faded.

I turned and looked.

The wall was on fire.

I went back to shooting zombies.

I heard Katrina crying in between shots.

I couldn't kill enough of them, but I had to protect her. I couldn't let her become like that little girl in the gas station. I couldn't let my promise to Randy be for naught.

The light behind me grew.

It made it harder to see the zombies.

Brad backed the Humvee closer to the wall, but not so close that it would topple on us. It gave me a little more room.

Wham.

Wham.

Wham, wham.

There were more than a dozen.

I'd already killed a dozen, yet they kept coming.

The sound of a shot rang out from behind me.

A zombie fell dead without my bullet in it.

I looked back, saw that the man, even with the fire below him, was taking aim at zombies.

The rear door on my left opened. Danny climbed out. He had a rifle.

He steadied it, aimed, fired.

Another zombie dropped.

Maybe we could survive.

"Just keep shooting," I said.

Wham.

Wham.

They dropped into the snow, one by one, but there were too many of them. The front kept advancing.

Sean came back to the Humvee, reached in.

He grabbed a gas can, then raced out in front of the Humvee and started pouring the diesel out in a line.

The zombies were advancing too fast, though.

"Sean, get back!" Brad shouted.

Sean didn't. He kept pouring.

A zombie reached for him, and he ducked out of the way. The zombie slipped in the snow.

Sean retreated.

He pulled out the flair gun.

Waited until the line of zombies had crossed his line of diesel.

He shot the flair into the fuel.

It lit.

The zombies caught fire. They burned, writhed in the flames. They went up like human torches. They fell over into the snow. The fire went out. They pushed themselves up again, blackened, but still alive.

I fired my gun into the zombies, again and again.

Sean turned to run back to the Humvee, but he slipped and fell in the snow.

I trained my gun on the zombies near him, shot them as quickly as I could, but they kept coming.

Sean tried to get back up, but a zombie lunged, grabbed his leg, pulled him back down to the ground.

"Sean!" I yelled.

I shot that zombie, but another one had already latched on to him.

He rolled over, kicked at them.

I couldn't kill them fast enough.

When the first bite landed on Sean, I knew it was over. I moved my gun just a little, and shot him in the head.

The flickers of the diesel in the snow grew lower and lower, though the light from the fire behind us grew and grew. I could feel the warmth on my back. The cold in my heart, however, grew.

"Danny, get back in," I shouted.

I shot and shot and shot.

The zombies fell.

The sounds of gunfire from behind me ebbed.

And then, by the combined light of the fire and my spotlight, I could find no more zombies to kill.

I looked down at Sean, laying on the ground, half a dozen zombies surrounding him in a circle where I'd dropped them.

It was the one I didn't kill that I regretted, the one that angered me.

I swung the gun around, pointed it at the man atop the flaming wall.

"You let us in, now," I shouted, "or I will take down this wall and let everything in."

24

The wall did have a door. I had missed it in the dark. There was only a crack where a whole section of the wall could swing open. The man atop the wall opened it for us, then came down to meet us with his hand out, nervously waiting for one of us to shake it.

"I'm Ike," he said.

Neither Brad, nor I, said a word. If he had just let us in when we first asked, Sean would have still been alive.

He went over to the fire and started shoveling snow onto it. After a few moments, Brad and I went to help him while Danny sat behind the big gun on top of the Humvee and watched for more zombies.

When we got the fire out, the wall was charred, but still stable.

We took Sean's body through the wall with us, tied out on the hood of the Humvee. It was too cold to bury him, so we found a spot that looked good, then tossed him over the side of the cliff like a burial at sea.

"We could use you," Ike said to me.

Brad put himself in between us. He must have seen my face go red with anger in the light of the Humvee headlamp. I certainly felt it.

"Not now, Ike," Brad said.

Brad surprised me with how calm he was. Sean had been our friend for three months, survived with us, helped us stay alive. If it wasn't for the piece of shit in front of us, he'd still be alive.

But Brad had a different agenda than I did.

"Did you see a woman and two men come through here in the last few days?" he asked.

"Nah, I only got sent up here yesterday," Ike said. "You could ask the commander, though. He's been up here for weeks."

"Commander? Where is he?"

I walked away, angry at Brad for getting in my way, and returned to the Humvee to check in on Katrina. She was quiet, asleep, but she felt hot. It was hard to tell, though, when everything else was so cold.

Brad came back from his chat with Ike. I saw Ike scaling the wall, again.

"Did you hurt him?" I asked.

"No," Brad said. "He was just following orders."

"Orders. Sean died because of him."

"I know, but we need their help. Killing him won't help find my step-mom or find a doctor for Katrina."

"They have a doctor?"

"Yeah. The commander *is* a doctor."

"Where is he?"

"Ike gave me directions."

"Then why aren't we driving, already?" I asked

Brad looked at me and grimaced, pondering saying something, I was sure, but he held his tongue.

We climbed in the Humvee, and Brad drove us off into the dark while I held on to Katrina. Minutes later, we pulled up to the camp.

Men stood up. Women, too. They had weapons out, but held down, not quite pointing at us.

I got out.

"We've got a little girl in here," I said. "She's hurt."

A man stepped forward, gray and bearded against the cold. "Hurt how," he asked.

"Broken leg."

"Not bit?"

"No."

He ran over to the Humvee, a look of concern on his face.

"Commander," someone called from behind him.

He ignored them.

"Where is she?"

"Passenger seat."

He opened the door, and I came around the front of the Humvee to help him, if necessary.

"She's lost a lot of blood," he said.

"We did the best we could," Brad said. "If your man had let us through, quicker."

"Sorry, we don't let anyone through at night. Hard to tell if they've been bit or not, and we're trying to keep this area free of the infection."

Then he looked up at Brad. "How *did* you get through?"

"We convinced Ike that it would be prudent," I said.

He looked at me. I don't know if I scared him or what. I had to look a mess.

"You can tell me later, or I'll wring it out of Ike. Help me get her to my tent."

Danny hopped out, while Brad stayed with the Humvee. He wasn't about to leave it alone when we didn't know exactly who these people were.

Danny and I helped the commander carry Katrina to his tent.

When we laid her down, he shooed us out, and suggested we get some rest.

"Will she be all right?" I asked before leaving.

"If you let me do my job," he said, "she should be, though she won't be going anywhere for a while."

"Good," I said. "Can I ask you one more question, first?"

"What?"

"We're lookin' for a group of three people that might have come through here in the last week. A woman, two men, probably well armed." I had never met Brad's step-mom. I couldn't describe her.

"There were a couple groups like that," he said. "We sent 'em on to the sanctuary. Now get out before this girl dies."

"Thank you," I said.

I let the flap on the tent close.

Sanctuary.

It sounded so good.

I walked Danny back to the Humvee. Brad had shut it off and was talking with a couple men in the camp.

"You say they're migrating?" one of the men asked.

"Yeah," Brad said. "Mostly south."

"Ahead of the winter?"

"No idea. If that's so, they didn't quite make it."

"Tell me something," I said as I arrived. "Why do you only leave one man up there on the wall at night?"

"There aren't enough of us to cover all of the blockades. Here, we're central to any of them if they need help," said a woman who I would have to say was no more than five feet in height. Her voice had the rasp of a long time smoker. "Besides, the zombies, they don't come up this way, mostly,"

"Mostly?" I asked.

"Yeah," said another man. "Most we see is a couple at a time, and the wall is so tall, no chance they can get over it."

"At least a hundred followed us up the highway," Brad said.

"I don't believe you," said the woman.

"Go ask Ike," I said. "Better yet, go stand guard with him. He might need your help."

"He'll be fine," the woman said. "If he has trouble, he'll shoot a flare into the sky."

I shivered. The chill was getting through my coat. I saw a fire burning a little ways away.

I turned away from the woman, took Danny's hand and pulled him with me toward the fire. I wasn't going to argue with her.

Brad followed a moment later.

Two men huddled around the fire. They moved to make room for us, and we knelt and warmed ourselves.

"The commander said a couple groups passed through that might have been your step-mother," I said.

"Where did they go?"

"He said they headed for Sanctuary."

"We've got to go, then," Brad said. He stood up.

"No, man, sit down," said one of the men at the fire. His eyebrows were black, his face ruddy from the heat of the fire. He was missing a couple teeth.

"I've got to go get them."

"No, man, you're stuck here. The road to Sanctuary is blocked by snows and avalanches."

"But Ike said he arrived yesterday," Brad said.

"See this snow coming down? It started last night. On the slopes the other side of the summit, it came down heavy, made the roads impassable, even with your Humvee."

"I could make it," he said.

I put my hand on his arm.

"Brad, we can't leave yet. Think about Katrina."

"But..."

"If they made it to Sanctuary, then they'll be there whenever we can make it through. If they didn't, there's nothing we could do anyway. They had three days on us, Brad."

He tried to withdraw from my grip, but his effort was anemic.

"Please, Brad. Sit down. Get warm. We'll find her when the road clears."

"She's right, you know," said the black-eyebrowed man. "And it's just the first snow of winter. The road could become passable in a week."

I don't think Brad believed it, but that didn't matter. He sat down, and we got warm together, and we waited with the men at the top of the mountain.

I thought of Sean, I thought of Randy and his family, and I thought of the little girl I had killed in the gas station.

But mostly, I thought about how good it was to still be alive with Brad at my side, and my two children, Danny, and now Katrina.

"Hey," I said, "Is any one of you a pastor?"

Right at that moment, a bright orange fire of a flare lit up the night sky, and the camp sprang into action.

It didn't bode well for my thoughts of getting married that night.

I looked at Brad.

He stared at me.

"You two going to help?" asked the black-eyebrowed man.

Together, we stood up. We didn't say anything. No words were needed. We followed the black-eyebrowed man away from the fire and back toward our battered Humvee.

"Wait for me," Danny said.

"Wouldn't leave without you," Brad said.

"We're like a zombie killing family, aren't we," Danny said.

I laughed, and hugged him to me.

"Yes we are," I said. "Yes we are."

About The Author

Mark Fassett lives in western Washington with his wife, children, and cats. He's a fantasy and science fiction author whose novels include *Shattered* and *Questioner's Shadow*. He's also written several novellas in those same genres. In the past, he had extensive experience in the mobile game business and was involved with some of the top selling titles at the time of their release, including multiple *Duke Nukem Mobile* games and *Guitar Hero World Tour Mobile*.

Find Me Online

Blog — http://www.markfassett.com
Twitter — http://twitter.com/mark_fassett
Facebook — http://www.facebook.com/markfassett.writer
E-Mail — mark.fassett@gmail.com

Learn About New Releases

Visit http://markfassett.com/newsletter to join my mailing list and get notified about my newest releases! I don't send out daily or weekly updates on my cat, and I don't tell you about my personal tragedies. I only send out information about new releases, and nothing more.